# THE PARADISE ROOM

The stone hut on the cliffs holds special memories for Nicole, who once spent so many happy hours within its walls — so when she has the chance to purchase it, she is ecstatic. Then the past catches up with her when Connor, the itinerant artist she fell in love with all those years ago, reappears in her life. But has his success changed him? And what of Daniel, the charismatic sculptor she has recently met? Nicole's heart finds itself torn between past and present . . .

*Books by Sheila Spencer-Smith*
*in the Linford Romance Library:*

THE PEBBLE BANK
A LOVE SO TRUE
THE BREAKING WAVE
LOVE IN A MIST

SHEILA SPENCER-SMITH

# THE PARADISE ROOM

*Complete and Unabridged*

# LINFORD
*Leicester*

First published in Great Britain in 2015

First Linford Edition
published 2016

A catalogue record for this book is available
from the British Library.

ISBN 978–1–4448–2840–5

Published by
F. A. Thorpe (Publishing)
Anstey, Leicestershire

Set by Words & Graphics Ltd.
Anstey, Leicestershire
Printed and bound in Great Britain by
T. J. International Ltd., Padstow, Cornwall

This book is printed on acid-free paper

# 1

'You've actually purchased a house down in Cornwall that you haven't set eyes on for ten years?'

Her friend looked so appalled that Nicole, kneeling on the floor of her Bristol flat, giggled.

'Annette, my friend, this is a very special house, let me tell you. My grandparents' old place, a cottage really. I couldn't believe it when I saw the photo in the *Western Morning News*, so I got onto the estate agent's website straight away and phoned them with my offer.'

'How special?' Annette sounded highly suspicious.

Nicole sprang to her feet in one graceful movement. 'Wouldn't a place be special to you if your happiest memories are of there? I downloaded the details so you could see. Here, take a look.'

Annette was still incredulous as she

accepted the sheet of paper and sat with her dark head bent as she read, her lips in a firm line of disapproval.

'So this is it?' she said at last, moving a little in the chair that was an uncomfortable fit for her large frame.

'This is it.'

Elated by what she had done, Nicole moved to the window and looked out at the busy street below. Though double glazing muted the sounds, she had grown used to the grinding of engines as vehicles climbed the steep hill. She was accustomed to the smell of fumes, too, when the window was open. But now they seemed magnified; as if, by thinking of what she was planning, her senses had sprung to life. She saw again the sunshine rippling across the bay, smelt the tarry seaweed clinging to the harbour wall and heard the gulls mewling overhead. Dark clouds came piling in sometimes, of course, and gale-force winds and rain too, but the cottage had withstood it all. That had been her world when she had come to live in Polvanion when she was fifteen.

And where she had fallen in love two years later.

She had been too immature then to know what was good for her. Now she was older and wanted a permanent home of her own. Somewhere peaceful to settle after years in the city running the catering business she had started when she left college. It was such a success now that it almost ran itself, and she knew of someone eager to buy her out. It was an opportunity not to be missed.

'I had such happy times there when I moved in with Gran and Grandpop, after Mum and Dad split up,' she said, her voice wistful. 'I lived there until I was seventeen.'

'But you can't go back to live there now and expect to take up where you left off. It's not possible. What are you going to live on, anyway?'

Nicole smiled. 'I expect something will turn up. I might even make use of that hut in the bit of land across the

lane in some way or other. Who knows?'
The stone hut that the artist Connor
Delaney had rented for the summer all
those years ago! Yes, why not?

They called it 'the hut', but in reality
it was a small stone building on its own
tiny plot of land. It had been used as a
haven for fishermen in the days when
the harbour down below had been a
bustling place, and not the sleepy
anchorage it later became. The building
stood proudly, looking out to sea right
across the bay to Chapel Head in the
dreamy distance. It was described as an
outhouse in the estate agent's details,
but it was far more to her than that.

Annette shrugged. 'I've heard some
crazy schemes in my time, but this
beats them all,' she said.

Nicole laughed as she came to sit
down near her friend. 'Credit me with
some sense, please, Annette. I've got an
appointment with the estate agent in
Truro tomorrow. They're short-staffed,
and so can't meet me at the property to
show me round, but I can have the key.

The house has been empty for ages.'

'So you're not legally committed yet?' Annette sounded more hopeful now.

'Only in my mind and heart.'

'You're impossible.'

Nicole looked with affection at her friend as she glanced again at the paper in her hand. She couldn't really hope to spark Annette's imagination in the same way as her own had leapt into action when she saw the house on Hunton and Bailey's website. Mr Bailey hadn't sounded at all astonished when she phoned to make an offer on the property without, as far as he knew, having seen it. He had got back to her quite quickly to say that the vendor had accepted because she wanted a quick sale.

'Why don't you come down to Polvanion with me, Annette?' she said. 'When you see it for yourself you'll realise what a wonderful bargain it is. How about it? Please say you will.'

Annette looked up in surprise. 'Tomorrow?' Her eyes had that dazed look and Nicole knew she was thinking hard, working out how it could be done.

'How long would we be away?'

'One night. Too far to do it in one day if I want a good look around the area. I haven't been back for years.'

'No, you haven't, have you.'

'I haven't booked in anywhere for the night, but that shouldn't be a problem this early in the year.'

'I'll think about it and get back to you,' Annette struggled to her feet and looked for somewhere to deposit the house details.

Nicole smiled, relieved her friend hadn't wanted to pursue the reason for her long absence from Polvanion. She would tell her one day; not now.

★ ★ ★

Seeing the cottage with its 'For Sale' sign attached to the white wall took Nicole by surprise, even though the property looked just the same as she remembered it, standing directly on the lane and staring out to sea. It was the end of a terrace of three, but you would hardly know it because the builder of long ago had made sure that each dwelling was different from the others. Cornerstone, Tamarisk Row, looked the proudest of the three, as if it wanted nothing to do with its neighbours.

Gran had smiled about that, especially as the other occupants were friendly enough to make up for the shortcomings of their dwellings.

'That it?' Annette said as Nicole drove slowly past.

'That's it.'

'Having second thoughts?'

'Memories, that's all.'

'Happy ones?'

Nicole sighed. 'I think so.'

She drove further along and then turned. There was just room to park the car in front of the cottage. They got out.

Inside, the building smelt musty. After the brightness of the sunny morning the dim light was depressing, and Nicole had sudden doubts about what she was doing. She knew the place had been empty for years, but she hadn't expected this gloomy atmosphere clinging everywhere.

Annette exclaimed in dismay at the kitchen at the back. 'The sink's disgusting,' she said. 'Although at least there's a cooker, even though it's in a filthy state. But just look at the floor!'

The place would need a lot doing to it, Nicole thought, but she would be able to afford to get someone in. She hadn't told anyone the exact amount of her godmother's legacy, just that it was enough to enable her to start a new life down in Cornwall.

'Or anywhere else,' Annette had pointed out, when she first heard about it.

'Cornwall,' Nicole had emphasised.

She could hear Annette's feet clattering on the bare floorboards overhead now, and hurried to join her.

'Not a bad view,' Annette admitted as they stood together at the front window, looking out at the stone building behind its low stone wall across the lane. Behind it, the sea twinkled in the sunshine.

They couldn't see the harbour down below, but Nicole knew it was there, a little to the left, where Connor had moored his boat. He had taken her out once or twice, and they had caught mackerel he'd gutted there and then. Scavenging gulls had swooped as he threw the remains overboard. One windy day, Nicole had thought she would be attacked by one particularly vicious-looking bird. Connor had laughed and told her he wouldn't let harm come to her ever, and she had believed him. He was only a year or two older than her, but so much more worldly-wise.

After a cursory look at the bedrooms and bathroom, Annette headed down to the kitchen again.

For a moment Nicole remained where she was and gazed round the empty room where her elderly grandparents had slept. She tried to remember how it had looked, with its green chenille bed-cover on the brass bedstead and the scent of lavender from the bottle on the bedside table that Gran always seemed to spill on the lace cloth.

They had been old-fashioned, she and Grandpop, proud of the values they upheld and strict in lots of ways, but she had loved them dearly. Her parents' divorce had shaken them badly. Alarm bells had rung at the developing friendship between their young granddaughter and the itinerant artist renting the stone hut, and that was that. Connor was out. He was gone so quickly she hardly had time to say goodbye, and she was packed off to make her home with her god-mother in Bristol. This, it was understood, was to give her a better opportunity to research suitable establishments to make sure of what she wanted to do before taking up a place at a catering college. It all sounded plausible, and yet . . .

Nicole took a last look round and followed Annette downstairs.

'I suppose the place could have some potential,' Annette admitted, her voice grudging.

10

Nicole smiled. 'Oodles of it.'

'If you say so.'

'Oh yes.'

They didn't stay long in the cottage after that because there wasn't much else to see.

'How about a spot of lunch?' Annette said as Nicole locked the door behind them.

Nicole indicated the stone hut in its tiny plot of land opposite.

'Just a quick look in there first?'

Annette shrugged. 'If you say so.'

They walked round the outside of the building first, keeping close to the wall because of the long grass and weeds. Annette, in front, stumbled over something. She yanked it up.

'It's a board,' she said. 'A 'For Sale' board.'

'Blown down by the wind, I should think,' Nicole said.

Annette put it down where she had found it, leaning against the wall. 'Looks like someone's placed it there deliberately.'

Nicole had reached the door in the front by now and was inserting the key in the lock. The door was hard to push open; it looked as if no one had tried for many long years.

Annette wrinkled her nose in disgust. 'A rubbish dump.'

That was exactly what it looked like, Nicole thought. Somewhere to store things no longer needed, just in case they came in useful one day, which were then forgotten or ignored when the last owners of the house moved away. And now everything was covered with dust and debris. It would need a good clear-out and several trips to the tip. But it was a good place, a private place, and she had spent happy days here.

She turned her back on the mess and went to the window that was so smeared with dirt and cobwebs it was like looking through grimy net curtains. The Paradise Room, Connor had called it, but it didn't look well-named now.

'You can see right across to Chapel

Head from here,' she said.

Behind her, Nicole could hear Annette rustling about among the piles of junk commenting on what she unearthed.

'What's this, Nicole?' she cried, pulling something out and holding it up. 'Who would want an old urn like this all covered in rust?'

'It was shiny-bright once,' Nicole said, turning round. 'For goodness' sake, put it down. You'll be covered in grime.'

Connor had used it for storing small pieces of driftwood for lighting the stove. Larger pieces were piled outside against the side wall near the tap that provided water. Sometimes only a thin trickle would come through and Connor, with a resigned shrug of his shoulders, would go off with a bucket to fill it from the tap outside the Post Office. After a bad storm it was always worthwhile to hike across to the beach on the other side of the harbour and to stagger back, laughing and happy, with armfuls of sea-washed planks and branches of trees that had somehow found themselves in the water.

Sometimes pieces of wood had tarry patches on them, and these had to be carried with great care if they didn't want to be covered in the stuff. It smelt good, though, all of it, once it was dry and crackling in the stove with the faint salty scent that made her cheeks glow and happiness steal round her heart.

The stove was still there, along with some of the wood, placed ready all those years ago and never used. A lump filled Nicole's throat as she looked at it, and she couldn't speak for a moment.

Annette pulled something out from a pile of crushed cardboard.

'Look at this rotten old canvas. What a mess.' Her friend's voice deepened with scorn. 'By the look of it the paint was splashed on in a fit of temper.'

'No.'

'What is it, then, a long-forgotten masterpiece?'

Nicole took if from her and placed it carefully beneath the window. 'You have to stand right back to make sense of it, and we can't do that in here with the state of the place. But when the place is legally mine I'll clear everything out. Then you'll be able to see what it is.'

Annette looked at her closely. 'You're upset.'

Nicole brushed her hand across her eyes. 'A bit. It's seeing it all again.'

'Then let's leave. We've been here long enough. It's a beautiful place, Nicole. Anyone can see that.'

This was a generous admission from her friend, who was plainly making an effort.

Nicole smiled at her. 'You and Tim will come and stay, won't you Annette, and see for yourself what Polvanion means to me?'

If she'd had doubts before, she had none now. This was what she wanted, this unique little building she hadn't thought about for years. The cottage, too, of course, but that was secondary.

Here in Polvanion she would settle.

# 2

'So, lunch?' Annette said hopefully.

Nicole took a last look behind her. 'After we've returned the keys,' she said as they went out through the gap in the wall and headed across the lane to the car.

'But that's back in Truro miles away, and it's getting late. Aren't you hungry, Nicole?'

'I can't relax until the keys are back in the office. Bear with me, Annette, please?'

Nicole's excitement had driven all thoughts of food from her mind, and she knew she was being unfair. All the same, she felt the return of the keys was something she must do. She would make it up to Annette later.

'You're bossy all of a sudden.'

Nicole smiled. 'Don't you feel focused on just one thing when there's some-thing important at stake?'

'So this really is important then, is it?'

'It is, oh it is.'

'Then let's go.'

'There's a bag of crisps in the glove pocket and some of those boiled sweets. Help yourself.'

'You're too kind.'

'And then after that we'll find somewhere really nice to eat, I promise.'

'I'll hold you to that.'

Her friend's voice sounded lighter now, her ill-humour fading as they set off.

Somehow, the way back didn't seem quite so long as the journey to Polvanion, and half an hour later Nicole was driving into the car park by the quay and pulling on the handbrake.

Hunton and Bailey's office was in Lemon Street. They opened the door and went in. On seeing them, Mr Bailey, looking flustered, got up from his desk.

'Ah, there you are, Miss, er . . . '

'Mallow,' Annette supplied.

'Miss Mallow. How did you find the place?'

Nicole smiled and handed him the keys. He dropped them on his desk as if they were red-hot.

'My offer still stands' she said.

He moved some papers from one side to the other, glanced at his laptop then directly at her and away again.

'I hope you weren't inconvenienced at all?

'Why should we be?'

'I . . . er . . . gave you the incorrect keyring. The one you should have had included keys to the outhouses at the back of the property. My mistake. I do apologise.'

'And the one at the front, the stone hut?'

'Well, you see, there's a problem there.'

'A problem?'

He looked unhappy. 'I should have mentioned it. Someone is keen to purchase that particular building as a separate unit.'

'To live in?' Annette demanded.

'There's never been planning permission for that. It isn't for sleeping in.'

'Then what does he want it for?'

'A local lad, a keen fisherman,' he said, ignoring her. 'Very keen. And the vendor is considering his offer.'

'But she can't do that,' Annette said indignantly. 'She's already accepted my friend's offer.'

Mr Bailey's thin shoulders slumped. 'I'm afraid she can. The buying and selling of property brings out the worst in people, as I expect you know.'

'We do now if we didn't before,' Annette said bitterly. 'This is totally unacceptable and I hope you told her so.'

'There's little we can do. I'm so sorry. We can act only under our client's instructions.'

Annette looked as if she would hit him, but Nicole put out a restraining hand. She was silent, thinking hard. Would she be prepared to increase her offer to include the stone hut?

'She's a horrible woman!' Annette sounded close to tears on Nicole's behalf.

Mr Bailey looked miserable. 'I'm afraid I can't comment on my client's personal attributes.'

'Can't you *do* anything?'

There was a moment's heavy silence as Mr Bailey struggled for a placating reply.

'He can pass on to his client my higher offer,' Nicole said. 'This very minute, please, while we wait.'

They both turned to look at her.

'Yes,' she said. 'I'm prepared to increase it on condition that the sale goes through quickly.'

Mr Bailey cleared his throat. 'This might change things a little, Miss . . . er, Mallow. May I know the figure you have in mind?'

He nodded as Nicole told him.

'Perhaps you'd care to take a seat while I telephone the vendor?'

There were chairs over by the window. Annette thumped down in the nearest and gave a huge sigh. Nicole suddenly felt cold, and she clenched her hands, trying to warm them, as she strained to listen to the one-sided conversation between Mr Bailey and the vendor.

Her knees felt weak when they left at last, and she leaned on the front windowsill outside for a moment to recover. Annette, too, looked shaken and still angry.

'Before you say anything,' Nicole said, 'I know what I'm doing.'

'You'd give in to that scheming woman?'

'I could have retired from the purchase if I'd chosen. It was my decision to go ahead. If I want the stone hut as well as the cottage, I've no choice.'

'But can you afford it?'

'I think so.'

'And now we've got to wait while she makes up her mind. We'd better move on. Our friend in there is looking anxious.'

They started walking back to the car, using the underpass to get to the other side of the busy main road.

'You want the place very badly,' Annette said, stating a fact rather than asking a question.

'Yes.'

'Then you have to get it.'

'We'll see.'

At the car they both paused and Nicole felt suddenly confident. 'I'll either get it or I won't,' she said. 'I've done all I can.'

'And a lot more than she deserves.'

'There used to be a place further down the river that did good food. Plenty of space to relax in while we wait.'

'Relax?' Annette said. 'You can think of relaxing? Why couldn't the woman make up her mind straight away?'

'She wants time to think about it. That's reasonable. Mr Bailey knows my mobile number. He's told her that it's a cash purchase, and that I want to know by four o'clock.'

'It's nearly that now.'

'Then let's go.'

Nicole had tried to appear calm but a mass of excitement, shock and determination were all swirling round inside her when Mr Bailey dropped his bombshell. It had all seemed so easy: viewing the property, discovering how much the stone hut as well as the cottage meant to her, and making the decision to go for it.

She could afford it, just, but the purchase and expenses involved in it would take care of most of the money at her disposal, with very little over for improvements. She had the feeling, though, that Christa would have approved of what she was doing.

She and her godmother had always been close. Christa, her father's dear friend from his student days, had been kindness itself to her all through her childhood. She had never married, and delighted in taking the young Nicole on special holidays every summer when she was growing up. Later, on one never-to-be-forgotten Easter visit when Nicole was seventeen and Christa was staying with them in Polvanion, she had tried to teach her godmother to sail.

'I'm just a landlubber,' Christa had said, hating it.

So on other occasions they had gone walking on Bodmin Moor instead, getting lost in mist one dreary day. Christa had produced two survival bags from her rucksack, and matches and kindling wrapped in polythene. Even though none of these things had actually been needed, because the mist soon lifted and there was no difficulty in finding their way, Nicole had been impressed by her forethought.

'That's what comes of me thinking of someone else for a change,' Christa had said cheerfully when they told her grandparents all about it on their return home.

As if Christa never thought of considering the wellbeing of others! All those undercover good works of hers testified to that. And so did her generosity to Nicole; both when she was growing up, and now, with this legacy that had made it possible for the purchase Nicole was about to make.

The rest of that Easter holiday had been spent in Polvanion. Christa had stayed on a little, not minding a bit entertaining herself when Nicole was busy helping Gran with the charity work in Truro she loved.

She missed Christa so much and always would. Maybe the stone hut and the use she made of it could be a memorial to her? She would work hard in restoring it all because Christa had loved staying with them that last summer. It would seem like a gift to someone she had loved who was no longer with her.

# 3

'You're smiling,' Annette accused Nicole as they got out of the car.

Annette looked round her, frowning, obviously unwilling to see any beauty anywhere, feeling as she did at the way things had turned out.

Around them were lawns and flower-beds of bright tulips and forget-me-nots looking peaceful in the drowsy after-noon sunshine. The Riverside Haven was still there, a small, low building covered in ivy, on the banks of the wide river that gleamed softly as it flowed past them to form the wide Fal estuary. On the opposite bank trees were beginning to come into leaf.

They sat outside at a picnic table to eat cheese-and-salad sandwiches and a huge amount of chips.

'That's better,' Annette said, wiping her mouth when they had finished.

Nicole sprang up.

'More coffee? I'm having some.'

She was halfway back with two steaming mugs on a tray when the mobile in her pocket rang. Her hands shook as she thumped the tray down on the table.

'Answer it!' Annette cried.

Nicole listened, bemused. 'Yes, my solicitor is in the picture,' she said. 'I'll notify him of the change in the offer. Yes, he'll be in touch. He'll get on to the vendor's solicitor straight away. Thank you.' She clicked off.

'Well?'

'I've got it.'

Annette let out a shriek, jumped up, waved her arms and then sat down again, laughing.

Nicole sank down in her seat and began to dry the bottom of the mugs with a paper napkin. She felt slightly sick. What had she done? With her increased offer on the property, her finances were going to be fully stretched.

'So Keen Local Lad is going to be

disappointed,' Annette said with relish. 'Serve him right.'

Nicole passed Annette's coffee to her with trembling hands and emptied the liquid she had split on the tray onto the grass.

'I shall have to get a job,' she said.

'You'll have one getting the place in order. You'll enjoy that, won't you, with that fabulous view? Anyone would pay good money to have that when they woke up each morning.'

'But a view doesn't pay the rent.'

'The rent? What are you talking about?' Annette's expression made Nicole laugh and her tension eased.

'All right then. Council tax, insurance, electricity bills, you name it.'

'There is all that, I suppose,' Annette conceded.

The view from the front windows was certainly fantastic, Nicole thought. It would make up for a lot.

'I know,' Annette said, sitting up straight. 'You could do Bed and Breakfasts.'

Nicole stared at her friend. 'You're brilliant, did you know that?'

Annette tried to look modest. 'Listen to the girl! I come all the way down here to look at some run-down building. I virtually go without lunch. I hear an outstanding offer made on that same property and she calls me brilliant. There's no sense to it.'

'You're not starving now,' Nicole pointed out.

'And neither will you be when you get that board hung up outside Cornerstone. People will be flocking to get booked in for the best B&B experience of their lives.'

Nicole laughed. 'I'll do my best.'

'You're serious?'

'Why not? It's a great idea. Thanks, Annette.'

Nicole's brain was working overtime. As soon as the contracts were signed and exchanged she would ask permission to start cleaning the house. By then she would have bought giant tins of paint, as much as she could afford.

She already had some left over from decorating her flat and could start with that as soon as the sale was completed. She took a sip of too-hot coffee, grimaced and put her mug down again.

'But don't you have to be inspected or something if you want to run a B&B?' Annette said.

'I don't know but I can find out. Do a bit of research. Contact the Tourist Board.'

'Who's your solicitor?'

'I'm using the one in Bristol who dealt with Christa's estate. He was so kind and efficient then. Yes, he's the one.'

'You'd better get on to him at once, then, before that woman changes her mind again. Keen Local Lad might get back to her and offer even more money. She's let you down once. She could do it again.'

Nicole looked at her in horror. 'You're right.'

'Then do it.'

'His number's back at my flat.'

Annette sighed. 'Let's get straight home tonight if you're up for it. That way you can contact him first thing tomorrow.'

'You're the best friend anyone ever had,' Nicole said humbly.

'Drink up, then, and let's get moving.'

'You'll be my first guest when there's a room ready, you and Tim. And we'll go out somewhere fantastic and have the best meal on offer.'

'And use up the profits before you have any?'

Nicole grinned. She felt full of vigour and optimism now and it was wonderful.

$\star$  $\star$  $\star$

Nicole was allowed inside the property just once before the completion date, to measure up for curtains and take another look round. She decided to make the most of it.

'That's because your vendor's afraid that Keen Local Lad will be on to you, bullying you to withdraw your offer so he can have that stone hut,' Annette said when Nicole told her.

'You think?'

'Definitely. He's probably out there in the bay even now in his fishing boat, watching for any sign of you turning up.'

Nicole had laughed, but she was a little wary as she drove through the village one windy Saturday in late April. She parked her car near the Post Office where the lane branched off to go down to the harbour.

*Let him make what he will of that, if he's watching,* she thought as she got out and checked her bag for the keys. Then she laughed at herself. Annette's paranoia about Keen Local Lad was getting to her too. She must stop it at once. But all the same she left her car where it was, because she wanted to walk the rest of the short distance on foot, as she had so often in the past, and recapture the feel of how it had been then.

The inside of the cottage didn't seem

so gloomy today because the doors to the kitchen had been left open and more light flooded the place. She suspected that her existing curtains would come in useful in the house, but measured the window frames in the front rooms to make sure. The two bedrooms with the view would have priority, of course. Her own at the back could wait for the moment as she wasn't overlooked.

These front rooms would need suitable floor coverings too. Cheap cord carpets might be the answer. Her budget would probably run to that, especially as she had a last-minute catering commission from one of her clients that would bring in extra cash. She had two single beds already, and that would do as a start for one of the guest bedrooms. A new double bed for the other? She would go into that later. Her old put-you-up would suit her needs for the time being, and she had plenty of bedding. The important thing was to make the rooms comfortable for prospective B&B guests. The shared bathroom might be a problem in these days of en suites, but she would hope for the best.

The kitchen next. She had brought Brillo pads and other cleaning things with her, and a large thermos of boiling water. Even with just that amount she managed to remove a lot of the gunge from the sink and the draining board. The cooker was another matter, but she dealt with some of the surface grime and was pleased with the result.

Time to go. She wiped her hands on her remaining dry cloth and stuffed it in her bag. A last look round and she was off.

At the car she hesitated. What next? She needed somewhere to eat her packed lunch, away from here in case she was being watched by Keen Local Lad out at sea. She was beginning to get ridiculously anxious about that. She thought of Annette back in Bristol and smiled.

She went into the building that was

half-shop, half-post-office, to ask the best way to reach the beach she could see in the distance by car. Two people turned to look at her.

'A fine morning in Paradise, m'dear,' said a burly man in a baggy navy jersey.

Nicole smiled. 'Oh, it is.'

He hitched up his left sleeve, revealing a mass of tattoos. 'Who'd want to be off to Spain when you can have all this?'

'My dad certainly wouldn't,' said the young girl with him. She gave him a sharp dig. 'Hurry up, Dad, and stop holding everyone up.'

He grinned down at her.

'That's enough, my lovely. Just showing a bit of friendliness to our new neighbour while I've got the chance. You know what your mum said. Let bygones be bygones.'

It was his turn to be served now, and when at last he had completed his business and they left, Nicole felt as if she had lost a friend. But 'let bygones be bygones'? What did he mean? This sounded intriguing, even slightly ominous. On the other hand, it was unlikely it had anything to do with her. She thought suddenly of something she had heard once, about never being able to return to the place you loved because you were looking for a past time as well as a location. But her past time was falling in love with Connor. She had grown up since then and wasn't looking for that. It was her own home she wanted, and with it a sense of security, because she knew the place of old.

'The beach?' said the cheerful woman behind the Post Office grille when Nicole asked. 'Penvenna, we call it. It's a long way round by road, m'dear. The best way is to use the car park on the other side of the village and walk down from there.'

'Car park?' said Nicole in surprise. 'Is that new?'

'It's been there for years, m'dear. You can't miss it. It's not far that way.'

Nicole thanked her and left. She must expect change, of course, but she wasn't too sure about a new car park, even if it was of use to her now.

Moments later she had parked beside some other vehicles and got out. Her lunch was packed in a small rucksack, which she heaved onto her back before setting off.

★　★　★

Out at sea, Daniel Logan shipped his oars and looked back at the coastline that, low in the water as he was in his small boat, seemed far away. He could make out the harbour plainly enough, and the houses on the hill, but he liked the feeling of being out-of-touch by his own choice. He liked, too, being his own master, working at his own pace as inspiration moved him. And it had been working overtime just lately, especially after the winter's storms had yielded such a rich harvest of driftwood for the taking. For relaxation today he had rowed himself out into the bay for a spot of fishing.

His boat rocked gently and the sunshine felt pleasantly warm. A glorious spring day, and one on which he should be roaming the beaches in search of the treasures the seas brought in at high tide, which provided relaxation from his more serious furniture restoration work. He needed more driftwood before the season got underway, even though his small workshop was overflowing with the items crafted from it that the tourists loved and paid good money for.

'So different,' they said. 'Such talent, seeing the potential in these odd bits of wood. Truly works of art.'

He had treasured such remarks. They helped prove that his strange way of making a living was not some aberration on his part, taken up purely to annoy his father. But why should he need to prove anything to himself when he knew in his heart that he was right? 'The family rebel' was how he'd been thought of when he gave up his law degree at university and came home to

Cornwall to take up this odd life. But why was he a 'rebel' simply for choosing to follow his own path, rather than someone else's idea of what he should do in life? Was Dad dubbed a 'rebel' by his own parents for choosing to go into law, instead of the family firm of boat-builders? An interesting thought.

So . . . space was at a premium if he wanted to work at full stretch. And that was why he needed bigger premises. He would have to do something about this before it was too late.

He glanced back at the land and sighed. He'd had a setback. No, a challenge. That was the way to look at it.

With sudden resolution he grabbed the oars and began to head back to shore. The mackerel weren't biting today and he was wasting his time out here.

# 4

To discover a wooden shack hidden away in the undergrowth of tall grasses and brambles halfway down the sandy path to the beach was a complete surprise to Nicole. And to find hot drinks and pasties on sale here was another. From further back, she had wondered why such a charming beach was empty this fine Saturday lunchtime. Now she knew. They were all here, seated on long benches by the wooden tables, tucking in to what smelt like a feast.

She smiled as she passed by. Her B&B guests would be pleased to hear about this too. She would make sure to mention it if they asked her about what Polvanion had to offer.

She saw now that there was a family sitting further along the beach behind some rocks where a stream wound its way to the sea. Three young children were busy damming it, bent over in concentration, sand flying.

The soft sand by the rock she chose to lean against was warm. She unpacked her rucksack and began to bite into the soft egg-and-cress sandwiches. Down at the water's edge she could see the gentle waves breaking, rolling a little way up the beach and then retreating again as if they didn't quite like what they saw. A few gulls hovered in the salt-laden air, and far away the misty headland she knew was Chapel Head looked mysterious.

She gave a sigh of pleasure, leaned back against the rock and closed her eyes.

A warning shout and loud squawking woke her suddenly. She looked up, alarmed, blinded by sunshine. Then she saw a man in a T-shirt and shorts looking down at her.

He broke into a grin and shrugged his shoulders.

'Sorry to startle you, but those gulls

were having a field day.'

She looked at her sandwich container, empty now apart from a piece of crust. She got to her feet, confused.

'I fell asleep.'

'The gulls don't miss a trick.'

She hurled the crust away from her as far as she could, and immediately a gull swooped. 'Greedy things.'

He laughed. 'I'll say.'

His mop of fair hair and deeply-tanned face made him look like a young god standing there in the sunshine with the sea at his back.

'I've been working hard,' she said in explanation, wanting him to know the reason for her lapse into unconsciousness.

'Me too,' he said. 'Beachcombing.'

'And that's work?'

'For me it is. I've been loading my van. And now I'm on my way to the Shack for sustenance. Looks like you need some too after losing your lunch. Care to join me?'

'I was going for a coffee.'

'Then off we go. I'm Daniel Logan. And you?'

'Nicole,' she said. 'Nicole Mallow.'

'Pretty name.'

She smiled with pleasure. There was something about him that exuded confidence, and it seemed perfectly natural to walk back across the beach with him, then up the sandy path to the wooden building.

Most of the customers had gone now, and he indicated a seat where they would have the best view over sea and sky. She put her rucksack down and joined him at the bar.

'Hi. Good to see you again, Daniel,' the girl behind it greeted him.

'I'm back for good now, Minna,' he told her.

A dimple appeared in her rosy cheeks as she smiled. 'We've been busy.'

'Good for you.'

'Dad's got a proposition to put to you.'

'Really?' He looked pleased.

She gave him a flick with a teaspoon.

'Not that. Behave yourself.'

'I never do anything else.'

'Says you.'

'Two coffees, please. Large ones. And a couple of those fantastic-smelling pasties.'

She looked at Nicole. 'Milk? Sugar?'

'Milk, please.'

'I'll bring it over.'

They sat down, one on either side of the table. From here Nicole could see the low headland that bounded the beach. She glanced behind her at the roofs of Polvanion in the distance, with the land rising behind the village. She could just pick out Tamarisk Row and the stone hut.

'So what brings you here to this lovely spot?' he asked.

'Just here for the day,' she said. 'I'm come down to . . .'

'Here we are, then. Enjoy.' The girl rattled the laden tray down between them and Nicole smiled her thanks.

The girl looked at Daniel. 'Is there anything else I can get you?'

'No thanks, Minna.'

'Salt, pepper?'

'No, really.'

She walked off, shoulders slumped.

Daniel picked up his pasty and bit into it. Nicole did the same, her eyes watering as the meaty steam met her eyes.

Daniel finished his first. 'That was great.'

'The best pasty I've ever tasted,' she said. 'Thank you. Are they homemade?'

'They're brought in ready to cook. Minna's parents tried several firms and they liked these best. Elliot's supply them from their place in St Austell. I was planning to eat here regularly if . . .'

The girl, Minna, was back.

'Something else?'

Daniel looked enquiringly at Nicole, who shook her head.

'That was delicious,' she said. 'But no thanks.'

Minna perched herself on the side of the table and looked at Daniel. 'So shall

I tell you Dad's bright idea?'

He smiled up at her.

'Go ahead.'

'You know what he's like, always looking to the future.' Her face clouded for a moment. 'Though for us here it's not great, right now.'

'That bad?'

'Afraid so. Anyway, he thinks you should sell some of your work here while you've got the chance. He'll fix up a special table over there. We can take the money from the sales for you. Your things will be quite safe. We'd take them inside every night when we lock up, of course. What d'you think?'

'Sounds good. In fact, it's more than good. I'm going to be pushed for space, after all. I'll need to get some of my stuff out of the way and this sounds perfect. Thanks, Minna. Tell your dad I'm grateful.'

A shadow crossed her face. 'It might make a difference, you see.'

The smile he gave her was one of encouragement.

'I'd like to think so.'

'Dad said we haven't a hope really. The council are adamant. The Shack's got to go, and it's just not fair.'

'It's a local amenity,' Daniel agreed. 'And I'd like to help. I know how it feels and it's not good.'

A meaningful look passed between them.

'So you didn't get it, then?' she said.

'Afraid not.'

'But why not?' Minna was indignant. 'The place should be yours. Everyone said so. You deserve it.'

'I was pipped at the post. It happens.'

'But not to someone like you, Daniel. You've lived here all your life and done so much for the community. You'll be doing something about it?'

He said nothing. His glance strayed to Nicole and she saw that he was looking over her shoulder at the village behind her.

For a moment, Nicole froze. It didn't take a genius to work out what they were talking about now.

47

Daniel was Keen Local Lad.

Horrified, she leapt up and said breathlessly that she must go, and thank you for the coffee and pasty, but she was late. He would think her incredibly abrupt but she didn't care. To think she'd been on the brink of telling him more than once why she was in Polvanion. She felt hot as she raced up the path, and then cold again with a nasty icy feeling sliding down her spine.

Annette would say that he had put in his own offer on the stone hut, knowing the vendor had already accepted one from someone else, and deserved not to get it. But that wasn't the consensus round here, it seemed. She was just an outsider coming down here and taking property from under the noses of local people.

* * *

Completion Day was two weeks later. Nicole had packed as much as she could but there was still plenty to think

48

about, especially as she was working until two days before the removal men were due. She hadn't much furniture of her own, but there was enough to get her started until the redecorating was done. She already had a double bed on order and had arranged for a carpet-fitter to come before it was delivered.

She spent her last night in Bristol with Annette and Tim in their Whitchurch home, glad to be out of the flat that didn't look like a home to her any more. Annette had offered to accompany her to Polvanion and help her get straight, but Nicole felt she needed to do this on her own and was grateful that her friend understood.

'At least you'll get a good night's sleep before you go, Nicole,' Annette said. 'And for this evening, Tim's booked a table at The Jolly Sailor for a slap-up meal to see you on your way.'

They were good friends to her, Annette and Tim. Once or twice it had been on the tip of her tongue to tell Annette that she had met Keen Local

Lad, but she had stopped herself in time. She didn't want to talk about Daniel and then listen to him being slagged off, as her friend's loyalty would demand.

Annette's eyes sparkled. 'And Tim's got a housewarming present for you.'

Intrigued, Nicole waited for her to fetch a bulky-looking parcel wrapped in a dustbin liner.

Annette plunged her hand in and whipped it out. 'What do you think?'

Nicole gazed at the beautifully-crafted varnished notice board on which the words 'Bed and Breakfast' were inscribed in gold paint. For a moment she was overcome. Then she sprang up and gave Annette and Tim huge hugs.

'It's simply great,' she said. 'You couldn't have given me a nicer present.'

'I'm working on a bracket for it as well,' Tim said gruffly.

'He'll be down to fix it for you the minute you're ready for visitors,' Annette promised.

Nicole was truly touched. She was

going to miss them a great deal. She and Annette had been at sixth-form college together for Nicole's last year, united in their dislike of the art lessons that Miss Pearson had insisted all the students should take as part of a rounded education. Annette had had no patience with any of it because any time not spent in hitting a ball about on the hockey field was, to her mind, a waste. Nicole, on the other hand, found it painful to look at any work of art because of Connor, and her anguish when her grandfather had sent him off so peremptorily.

She slept well that night and woke refreshed, ready to set out for what she hoped was the best decision she had made so far in her life.

# 5

Daylight was fading fast and across the sea a rosy band reached nearly to the far headland and then faded. It would soon be dark. A distant light flickered and then was gone. Exhausted with the events of the day, Nicole gazed out of a front bedroom window until there was little to see.

She had arrived here well in advance of the removal van, switching on the immersion heater in the airing cupboard as soon as she had checked that the electricity and water were turned on as promised. Once she had used up the hot water from the flask she had brought with her, there was plenty on hand for making a start on washing down the walls of this room — after she had ripped up the disgusting-looking underlay that covered the floor in the front room downstairs. By the time the van came lumbering up it was done.

Thank goodness there were TV points in both the front bedrooms as well as the room downstairs. That was one fewer expense to face. She needed broadband, of course, and must make enquiries about that as soon as possible.

The removal men hadn't taken long to unload, and by lunchtime her furniture was all in place to her satisfaction and she had washed the tiles on the kitchen floor. She spread some colourful bedspreads on the two single beds to make one room look presentable, even though they wouldn't be made up with the rest of the bedding until the room was redecorated and carpeted.

Lunch was the packed one Annette had provided, and Nicole ate it at the table in the kitchen. She had made sure her electric kettle was packed in her bag with tea, coffee and milk, so a hot drink was no problem. After that she tackled the cooker until it was as clean as she could get it, wiped down the shelves in the kitchen wall cupboard above, and then began on the boxes piled on the sitting room floor.

Now it was time to relax a little and leave the rest till next day. She was surprised that there was no sound from her neighbours; she had even tapped on the adjoining cottage door earlier, but got no answer. There hadn't been anyone around when last she was here, either.

She had thought that she might wander around a bit and find something to eat before dusk descended but, tired as she was, this had seemed too much trouble. So she had a long soak in the bath instead, slipped on an old tracksuit, and then opened a tin of baked beans to eat cold with some of the loaf of bread she had brought with her.

Now, refreshed after two mugs of tea, she turned away from the window, sank down on the sofa and closed her eyes.

Sunshine streaming in greeted her when she opened her eyes early next morning. Shivering, she leapt up, aware that she had been on the sofa all night and was now stiff and hungry. In the kitchen she plugged in the kettle and looked in frustration at the gas hob. She had believed she had thought of everything but here was one thing that had defeated her. Matches! On her previous brief visit the cleaning had taken priority and it hadn't occurred to her to check the rings on the cooker. She had found out to her cost last evening that matches were required to light them. So, for the moment, no cooked breakfast to fill the gap gnawing at her insides. Bread and butter it would have to be, and then a quick shower and change of clothes.

★　★　★

'Holiday lets now, all them along there,' Mrs Pascoe in the Post Office told her when Nicole, dressed now in jeans and jersey, called in soon after nine. 'No one there now, m'dear, not till next week.'

No wonder there had been such silence, Nicole thought as she returned to Cornerstone with three packets of matches. Ten minutes later, she sat down to a plate of bacon, egg and baked beans, and felt a great deal better.

By lunchtime she had loaded her car with the horrible underlay and all the empty boxes. A trip to the tip was imperative; if only she knew where it was! Once again, she upbraided herself for her lack of forethought in not enquiring about this, especially as the stone hut was full of stuff she needed to dispose of. Another visit to Mrs Pascoe and her Post Office shop for information?

This time she was disappointed to find it closed.

'Saturday afternoon closing,' said a young voice behind her.

She swung round to see a girl in jeans and sleeveless top looking at her expectantly. She saw now that it was the same young person whose lingering father had been ahead of her at the Post Office counter yesterday. Her astonishment at seeing her standing there kept Nicole silent for a moment.

'Want some help?' said the girl. 'Dad said you would. Sophie Penberthy, that's me.'

'Oh,' Nicole said. 'I just wanted to ask about something.'

'I might know.'

'The nearest refuse tip. Any ideas?'

The girl's eyes lit up. 'It's not far. I'll show you if you like.'

The offer was too good to refuse.

As Nicole had hoped, the rough cord matting she remembered from long ago was still in place on the floor of the stone hut. She had forgotten about it on her visit with Annette to view the property. In any case, they hadn't disturbed any of the stuff covering it; except, of course, for unearthing the brass pot and the canvas that somehow had got left behind when Connor had to leave so quickly. After he had gone she hadn't come into the hut again before her own departure to make her home with Christa in Bristol.

But now, with some of the objects heaved aside thanks to the help of her surprising new friend, she could see what lay beneath her feet.

And so they started to move some of the stuff to the door of the hut. There was room in her car for more than Nicole had thought, and she was glad of the help with loading.

'I'm going to need a good few runs to the tip,' she said, rubbing her dusty hands down the sides of her jeans.

'There's all those canvases over there,' said Sophie. 'D'you want those to go too?' She pulled aside a ragged sheet covering them. 'Too good to chuck?'

Nicole thought of the painting Annette had found; now here were more of them. She hesitated. Useless or of great value? She had checked on the Internet before she left her flat, unable to resist. Connor was now a member of the RA and having solo exhibitions in prestigious London galleries. There was even a bit about a national tour being set up.

'I knew the artist once,' she said.

'You did?' said Sophie, her voice full of excitement. 'Romantic. D'you know where he is now? He might want them back.'

Nicole smiled. 'Unlikely. But I'll hang on to them for old time's sake.'

Sophie placed the sheet over them again with great care.

'D'you know many people round here?'

'I don't think so. Not now. I met someone the other week. Daniel Logan.'

'Oh, him,' Sophie's disparaging tone of voice spoke volumes.

'You don't like him?'

'He's my mum's cousin.'

Nicole hid a smile. Daniel was good-looking in a boyish kind of way, his wide-apart grey eyes seeming interested in whatever he saw. Anyone could fall under his easy charm. She might even have done so herself if she hadn't known who he was and been immediately on her guard.

'And your mother?' she said. 'Does she not approve of Daniel either?'

Sophie hesitated. 'Who said anyone else didn't?'

'You've got me there.'

Sophie shrugged and tuned away. 'What about the rest of this rubbish, then? Do we dispose of the lot?'

'I think so.'

'Where did it all come from?'

'The previous owners must have stored it here and then forgotten about it. My grandparents were here before that. You'd have been too young to know them.'

'Dad did. And Mum, when they were first married. They lived up at Back-Along then, until I came along.'

Here was the feeling of homecoming she so wanted! Tenuous, Nicole knew, but there all the same; a tiny line to her previous life that was valuable now she had come back to live in Polvanion.

'I'd like to meet your Mum and Dad,' she said.

'You met my dad, Joe, in the Post Office.'

Burley Man, of course. 'So I did. And where do you live now?'

'Over at Treloose.'

'And you're still at school?'

'I'll be sixteen next month.'

Not much younger than she herself had been when Connor took up residence for the summer here in the stone hut, Nicole thought. She glanced at the sheet-covered canvases.

'Let's go,' she said.

The refuse place was further than Nicole had anticipated but it didn't matter. She enjoyed the drive along high-banked lanes, with glimpses of the sun-dappled sea on their right. When they reached the main road the driving was easier, but she was still glad of Sophie's directions.

On the way back Sophie broached something that had obviously been on her mind since they set out. 'I need a part-time job,' she said.

'You do?'

Sophie moved uncomfortably in her seat. 'I'm not trying anything on, honestly. Dad warned me not to. You won't tell him?'

Nicole smiled. 'That you very kindly offered to help me load my car? Of course not, if that's what you want. How long have you been looking?'

'There's nothing much round here. I've tried.'

She sounded so forlorn that Nicole was touched. They reached the turning to Polvanion and Nicole slowed down

'I could offer you work for the rest of today, Sophie, but I'm afraid that's all until my finances improve.'

Sophie still sounded unhappy. 'Mum thinks I should steer clear for the time being.'

Steer clear? That didn't sound good. Unfriendly, in fact. There was plenty to think about here.

Nicole drove slowly round the last bend. 'So are you on for the rest of the afternoon if I pay you from now, Sophie?'

The girl brightened. 'If you're sure.'

'There's still masses to take to the tip.'

They made two more journeys and

the stone hut was looking more spacious by the time they had done that. Nicole paid Sophie what she considered a reasonable wage.

'So how will you make your finances improve?' Sophie asked as they left the stone hut and went into the lane.

'Bed and Breakfasts,' said Nicole. 'As soon as I've got the place in order I shall look into it. Do you think it's a good idea?'

'Why not? We get a lot of people here in summer. It used to be a B&B a long time ago.'

'It did?' This was interesting.

'There was a sign board hanging out from the side wall. Up there. Can you see where it went?'

Nicole looked to where Sophie pointed and could just make out the small holes on the wall where a bracket had hung.

'Thanks Sophie, you've been a great help to me,' she said.

If Cornerstone had been used for the purpose once before, surely that would indicate it could be again? Unless, of course, the powers that be considered that there were enough such businesses in Polvanion already. She didn't yet know how such things worked. This evening she would take a walk round the place to check how many boards she could spot. It would be a start, anyway, if hardly a professional one.

# 6

Nicole stood on the edge of the car park high up above the sea where she had parked the day she came to Polvanion to measure up. There were still two cars here, their owners presumably holidaymakers on the beach enjoying the rest of the day. She wished, suddenly, that she was doing the same. What was she doing counting B&B boards hoping they would tell her something about the advisability of setting up her own business in the same way? She had been working too hard and now she had lost the ability to think straight.

The evening was so calm that the sea was like a delicate painting on pale blue silk. Not a ripple disturbed the surface and only on the horizon was it a deeper shade of blue. A lonely gull flew slowly across the sky and to her right the boats at rest in the harbour down below were motionless.

She had set out earlier on her self-imposed task with a light heart, climbing the hill to the top of the village, intending to work her way along and then down so that she covered most of the streets. It occurred to her only then that some B&B establishments might choose not to have a board swinging from their property.

In any case, Cornerstone was far from ready to receive guests. She had only just moved in, for goodness' sake, and she couldn't expect miracles. Tomorrow she would start painting the two front bedroom walls and make a start on preparing the front room downstairs, previously a sitting room, for the same treatment. This was to be the guests' dining room. By the end of the week the carpet-fitter would have done his work and the telephone line reconnected.

There was a movement far out on the sea now, and as she watched she saw a boat approaching. The drone of the engine carried across the still water as it headed for the harbour. By the time she walked down the hill to the village square, there was silence again apart from the mewling of a gull somewhere overhead and the distant bark of a dog. She made her way down the slope and saw Daniel standing up in his newly-arrived boat, now attached to the quay.

He waved. 'Hi there.'

Too late to turn back. Joining him, she looked in surprise at the oddly-shaped pieces of wood in the bottom of the boat.

'So you haven't been fishing?' she said.

'I have, but not for fish.'

'I thought you were a fisherman, a keen one, by all accounts.'

He looked at her oddly. 'Someone been talking?'

'No, I . . . it's not a secret, is it?'

He laughed. 'Apparently not.'

He picked up an armful of driftwood and climbed up the steps to the quay.

'I go fishing quite often, as it happens, like a lot of people. It's relaxing and I need that sometimes. How are you settling in?'

'It's quiet round here.'

He placed his cargo carefully by the wall and returned to the boat for more.

'Make the most of it before the season gets underway,' he said, looking up at her. 'If you want to know what's going on take a look at the village notice board. Have you seen it?'

She shook her head. 'I haven't done much except go to the tip.'

'Throwing your belongings away already?'

She could see he was joking by the upward tilt of his eyebrows.

'Hardly. There's a lot to clear out.'

'From the stone hut?'

What was the use of pretending, she thought, when he must know who she was?

'Well, you know what's in there, I expect?'

Busy with his wood he was back up now on the quay with the rest of it.

'You could say that.'

'I'd had my offer accepted before you

made yours,' she pointed out.

He looked at her keenly. 'If you say so.'

'I do say so.'

'I did a bit of work for Mrs Benton before I set off for Australia. I always understood she would give me first refusal.'

'I see.'

This was no fault of hers, but she could understand his sense of betrayal when he got back and discovered the promise had been forgotten. Or maybe Mrs Benton had thought she would get a better deal with someone else. It was because of Daniel that Nicole had had to increase her own offer on the property. By rights she should be annoyed with him, but instead she felt a rush of sympathy.

'I'm sorry,' she said.

He gave a hollow laugh. 'I'd like to believe it.'

She wanted to make him understand her own reason for purchasing the place, but he gave her no chance. He was back in the boat again, pulling out a tarpaulin and coming back up to cover his stack of wood, obviously engrossed in making it safe and not wanting to be interrupted.

At last he straightened. 'I'd take a look at the notice board if I were you,' he said.

This was obviously a dismissal but he sounded friendlier now.

'I will.'

He nodded as he looked critically at his covered pile of driftwood. 'I'm in a bit of a hurry. An appointment in St Austell to pick up some supplies I ordered. See you.'

And he was off. A brush-off? It was very much like it. Her previous optimism gave a downward lurch. She felt oddly upset, but that was stupid. Hadn't she determined to keep well clear of him?

On the far side of the village square she saw it: a large board behind glass fastened to a sturdy wall. She went closer to look. The times of church services in the parish, the speaker at the next WI meeting, a keep-fit class in the Victory Hall — wherever that might be. There was a notice of the Garden Club outing to Rosemoor in Devon in June. At the top-right-hand corner was a smaller notice announcing a forthcoming series of exhibitions at the prestigious Melrose Art Gallery in Truro. Nicole turned away. It was useful to know what the inhabitants found interesting without feeling the need to take part herself.

She was pleased with her progress in the days that followed, and found herself upstairs admiring the two front bedrooms more often than was necessary. Tim had promised to fix new curtain rails for her when he and Annette arrived for their promised visit next weekend.

On Wednesday she was up early ready for the carpet-fitter. She had expected him to come, as promised, soon after eight o'clock, and it was now nine. It was hard to settle to anything else. By ten it was obvious that he wasn't coming. She picked up his card from the kitchen windowsill and went down to the Post Office to phone.

His visit had been cancelled by someone.

'The day before yesterday,' the person on the other end said. 'I took the call myself. So he re-scheduled, you see. I know the diary's pretty full, but I'll give him a call on his mobile and he can get back to you. I'm sorry for the confusion, m'dear.'

This was a blow Nicole hadn't foreseen. Mrs Pascoe was busy at the counter or she might have confided in her. She emerged into the fresh air and stood gazing down at the harbour, deep in thought.

Daniel's boat was still there, tied up to the harbour wall, but there was no sign of him. She felt a sudden urge to confront him and demand to know if he'd had a hand in the cancellation. Then she turned away. She would do something positive and not let her feelings get the better of her. From what she had seen of Daniel he didn't seem the sort of person to do something so underhand.

It was no use hanging round here waiting for a call on her mobile when she couldn't get a signal. There was shopping to do. She would go to Truro.

* * *

The impressive facade of the Melrose Gallery in Lamb Street sported carved stone vine leaves intertwined with shepherds' crooks and sea shells. A unique combination, Nicole thought, as she stood looking up at it. At street level, down to earth after the fantasy above, was a large glass case featuring notices of forthcoming exhibitions. The most prestigious of these, it seemed, was a series featuring well-known artists, all of them with strong connections to Cornwall.

Intrigued, she moved closer. Connor Delaney . . . the name jumped out at her.

She had been thinking of him a lot since discovering the canvases, so she could be imagining things. But no, there it was: 'Connor Delaney', in bright gold lettering on a black background that brought an image of the man himself instantly to mind. She thought of the man he had been ten years ago when he wore his wavy hair to his shoulders and despised any clothing but old T-shirts and baggy shorts. But the intervening years would have altered that. He was well-known now, and an artist — but with strong connections to Cornwall? She didn't think so. Maybe the other artists hadn't much connection either, and it was all a big con.

Smiling, Nicole pushed open the door. At the desk at the far end of the foyer a thin woman with purple fingernails peered at her from over her glasses. A nametag on the lapel of her jacket announced her to be Miss A. Burden.

'We're closed for refurbishing,' she said.

Nicole moved closer. 'I'm enquiring about a forthcoming exhibition.'

'Ah, an exhibition.' Miss Burden rummaged in a drawer. 'Any particular one?'

'Connor Delaney?'

She drew out a list and pursed her lips. 'We haven't had Connor Delaney before. Unreliable, so I'm informed. The week after is Kirk Andrews. Now *he's* good if you like atmospheric seascapes. The best.'

'Connor Delaney is good too.'

'You know him?'

'I know his work.'

'Seascapes?'

Nicole shook her head. 'Not that I know of. He used not to.' In fact Connor had made his opinion of them only too plain. Not for him the obvious choice for an artist choosing to live on the edge of the sea. He liked vigorous colour, slapped on in such a way that onlookers were unable to recognise his chosen subjects of interiors of caves, caverns beneath the sea or dark forests without standing well back. He used the shoreline and cliffs for his inspiration but no one would guess. Just occasionally he would portray the surroundings in recognisable form, and she had come to appreciate the rare occasions when this happened.

'Two weeks from the tenth of May is Connor Delaney's slot,' Miss Burden said, in a final tone of voice as if she were wasting time answering enquiries about such things. 'Local, are you?'

'From Polvanion.'

'Then you qualify for a preview invitation for the evening of the ninth, and you'll have the chance to speak to the artist.'

In her pocket Nicole's phone rang.

'Oh, please excuse me,' she said, rummaging for it.

Miss Burden waited in pained silence while Nicole listened to the apologies from the carpet-fitter on the other end of the phone. He could fit her in on the ninth of May at the earliest, but not after that until the middle of the month.

Nicole clicked off. 'I have an appointment on the morning of the ninth of May,' she said.

'You'll find that the Preview Evening is in the evening,' Miss Burden said coldly.

'Well, yes, it would be,' said Nicole humbly.

'I'll need to take your phone number if you would like an invitation.'

'Of course.' This was the easy solution to finding out what she should do with Connor's discarded paintings. 'It will have to be my mobile number. I'm not connected to a landline yet.'

Miss Burden permitted herself a brief smile as she took her details and handed her the invitation.

'Please feel free to bring a guest.'

Nicole was glad she had completed her shopping as soon as she arrived in Truro. The prospect of meeting Connor face to face again might have driven the necessity from her mind. She glowed with satisfaction as she walked back to the car.

★　★　★

Annette and Tim arrived early on Saturday morning. Annette enthused about everything she saw, as if it had been her idea in the first place for Nicole to move down here. Tim, more cautious, looked round with pleasure but said little.

Nicole laughed. 'I'm expecting her to pick up on any flaws I haven't thought of yet.'

Annette wrinkled her nose. 'It all smells so fresh and clean.'

Tim looked at his wife fondly. 'Surely not a flaw?'

Smiling, Nicole leaned back in her chair. It was good to have her friends here; she was looking forward to showing them round the area, with a pasty lunch at the Shack behind the beach, and a meal out this evening at the Penvenna Hotel along the coast. This had been recommended to her by the elderly couple who had arrived today at the cottage next door for their annual holiday.

But first Tim had work to do. While he was fixing the curtain rails in the three bedrooms and dining room,

Nicola took Annette for a stroll round the village, laughing at the way her friend puffed her way up the hill from the harbour to the square. They sat down for a rest on the seat at the end of the car park, and looked out over the sea and the headlands in the distance. Annette dabbed her moist brow with a tissue and heaved a sigh of relief.

'I wouldn't want to do that too often,' she said. 'But it's worth it for the fantastic view.'

Nicole smiled. 'I try not to waste time looking at it too often. Too much work to do.'

'You've done wonders, Nicole. I'm impressed. But you won't overdo it, will you? You need time off as well, you know.'

Nicole didn't answer for a moment. How could she explain the tug at her heart when she woke each morning to the realisation that she was back in a place that had meant so much to her?

'Do you remember me telling you once about the artist I got to know when I was living here?' she said at last.

'Just before you moved to Bristol?'

'I'm going to be meeting him again on Monday.' Nicole tried to hide the tremor in her voice but made a bad job of it.'

Annette looked at her in dawning realisation. 'That's the man you were in love with all those years ago?'

'Or thought I was.'

'And now?'

'Of course not.'

'And he's agreed to meet you?'

'You sound suspicious.'

'You're not expecting to start something up again?'

'I've got a ticket for the Preview Evening for his exhibition, that's all. He'll be there talking to people. I don't suppose he'll recognise me.'

'But you'll recognise him?'

'It'll be obvious who he is. I've unearthed some more of his paintings in the stone hut. He might be interested in having them back. What's the harm in that?'

'As long as he doesn't try anything on.'

'For goodness' sake, Annette, what is this? I thought you were my friend.'

'That's why I'm concerned.'

★　★　★

Later, at the Shack, seated on one of the long benches eating pasties, Annette seemed to have regained her good temper. She gave a sigh of pure pleasure. 'It's so beautiful here.'

'You approve, then?' Nicole asked, knowing the answer would be yes. Even Tim was smiling and relaxed.

'So,' said Annette, sitting upright and wiping her sleeve across her mouth. 'Have you taken any bookings yet?'

'I've contacted the Tourist Board and they've been helpful. When I get broadband sorted I'll get listed on TripAdvisor and various websites for finding B&Bs. I have to arrange for insurance cover too.'

'And you'll need to set up your own website,' said Tim. 'I can help you with that, and with your accounts too, since it's my job.'

'That's really kind,' she said. 'I need to get food and safety standard certificates too. I'll probably be inspected at some point.'

Annette laughed.

'No problem there with your qualifications, surely? The kitchen looks a dream after all your hard work.'

Nicole flushed, pleased that Annette approved.

'They'll all love it here,' Annette said.

'If the carpet-fitter turns up.'

'That was a bad business.' Tim looked thoughtful. 'And you've no idea who could have done such a thing?'

Nicole shook her head. Her anger had faded now, leaving a dull ache because there was someone out there who didn't want her here. She wasn't used to being disliked, and not knowing who had contacted the firm on her behalf made it worse. The only person she could think of was Daniel's friend, Minna, but storming up to the Shack now to confront her could be disastrous.

'I'll just have to ignore it,' she said

'And have something like that happen again?'

There was that, of course, but what could she do?

# 7

Nicole dressed as carefully for the Preview Evening as she had for the dinner at the hotel with Annette and Tim. She allowed herself plenty of time to drive the fifteen winding miles to Truro and parked this time behind the gallery. There were no other cars there yet, and she chose a spot as near to the entrance as she could, so that it would be easy to collect Connor's paintings from the car should she need to.

She got out carefully and straightened the skirt of her dress, hoping that sitting in the car hadn't creased it.

The evening was peaceful, with just the hint of misty pinkish sky above the buildings that seemed to promise more of the same tomorrow. She wondered whether to stroll through the quiet streets until the preview had got well and truly started and she had the chance of viewing Connor among the crowd before he saw her.

Another car came swerving through the car park entrance and screeched to a halt as she emerged near the entrance to the gallery. From it sprang two young men in football attire. Still shaken by the closeness of the encounter, Nicole stood back against the wall to regain her composure and watched as they strode purposely off through the gateway towards town. Not clients for the preview, then.

She glanced at her watch. This silence now they had gone was strange. Could she have got the wrong evening? The main door was closed, when surely by now it should have been wide open to welcome people inside.

Nicole stared at the small notice attached to the wooden panel at one side of the door with a feeling of disbelief. With regret, the advertised exhibition had been cancelled at short notice and preview ticket holders informed.

For a few stupefied moments she stared at it. So much for that, then. She wouldn't see Connor after all. It was just as well she hadn't invited Sophie Penberthy to come with her; although now, of course, they wouldn't have been as late back as she had expected. For that reason she had hesitated to pass on the invitation, knowing that Sophie had school the following day and her parents might have vetoed it anyway.

She hardly knew how she felt as she drove away from Truro back along those narrow lanes she had set out on earlier in such anticipation. Disappointed, of course, because of the paintings in the boot of the car she would have liked to return to their rightful owner. She had been looking forward to meeting new people, too. But there was nothing to be done but to return to Cornerstone and admire the new carpets in the bedrooms and dining room. The carpet-fitter had done a good job, and with the windows now curtained the rooms looked attractive and welcoming.

But after her disappointment, this didn't seem enough.

She parked her car in the place she used now, further along the lane, and walked the short distance to Cornerstone, carrying the paintings. Inside the stone hut, she placed them carefully against the far wall, and then stood back to look at them as if she were seeing them for the first time.

They were good. Too good to lie forgotten here. Connor had said at the time that his works were his children. Did you forget your children after ten years? She didn't think so. He put so much concentration and emotion into each of his paintings. They had been his lifeblood then, and she suspected it was the same now.

Her initial surprise and dismay at not seeing him this evening after all had put most other things out of her mind, and she hadn't even wondered at the reason for the cancellation. He must have been working towards his output for the exhibition for months. So what did that make her . . . ? Selfish, of course, thinking only of her own feelings when Connor might have been involved in an accident serious enough to warrant cancellation. But in that case, surely the gallery would have given that as the reason?

On impulse, she picked up one of the paintings and held it close to her for a long moment. Then, reluctant to be parted from it, she took it out with her. Outside the next-door cottage, fumbling with the key in the lock, was the elderly couple she knew from this morning as Mary and Ken.

Mary's pleasant face lit up on seeing her. 'What have you got there, dear?'

'You must forgive my wife,' Ken said, leaning a little on his walking stick.

'Forgive?' Mary said in mock annoyance. 'For what, may I ask?'

He looked at her tenderly, and then turned to Nicole with a slow smile that made him seem much younger than the eighty years she knew he was.

'For your curiosity, my dear; your

burning desire to know everything about everybody.'

'Interest. That's what it is. Interest.'

'And it's not a secret,' said Nicole, smiling too. 'It's the work of an artist who rented the stone hut from my grandparents one summer long ago.'

'And you knew him?'

'I was fond of him.'

'And you were very young?'

Ken looked disapprovingly at his wife. 'That's enough, my dear. We mustn't keep the poor girl talking here. I expect she has things to do.'

'Not this evening,' said Nicole. 'Not any more. I've just had a wasted journey into Truro, I'm afraid. The artist's exhibition preview was cancelled, and I didn't know — I don't get a mobile signal here, and I didn't think to check for voicemail.'

'That's too bad,' said Mary with sympathy. 'What do you say to joining us for a while and telling us all about it? Ken makes a good cup of coffee, and we've a new tin of biscuits that needs opening. I'd love to take a closer look at that painting, too.'

Nicole accepted with pleasure. She was tired and discouraged, and the thought of spending some time with these kind people was appealing.

Their cottage was much smaller than Cornerstone and was open-plan on the ground floor. The surrounding scent of lavender was pleasant, and Nicole saw that a dish of it stood on the front windowsill.

'Perfect for a holiday place,' said Mary. 'We've been coming here for many years now. The only thing is, it only sleeps only two.'

'I'm lucky my place has three bed-rooms,' said Nicole as she sank down into the comfortable chair Ken pulled forward for her. 'Now it's carpeted, they look really nice.'

Mary wanted to know about the colour schemes and the pattern of the curtains, and while Ken made the coffee Nicole told her of her Bed and Breakfast plans.

'I already have the notice board to fix

up outside,' she said with pride.

Not only Mary but Ken was deeply interested in hearing this. They had friends, younger than themselves, they told her, who wanted to come and see them while they were here, and what better way was there than for them to book in for a few nights next door with Nicole?

Flushed with pleasure, Nicole explained that she wasn't yet up and running, but Mary and Ken would have none of it.

'From what you tell us, your place sounds delightful,' he said. 'What does it matter if you haven't been inspected and whatever? So convenient for us.'

Smiling, Nicole let herself be persuaded. Mary put down her empty cup and leaned forward.

'And now that's settled, can we see your painting?'

* * *

The first thing that Nicole did next day, once her landline had been connected, was to phone the Melrose Gallery. This was Mary's idea, and one that she should have thought of for herself — probably would have done, given time.

She had been gratified by the couple's appreciation of Connor's work. Mary had seen at once that the myriad of bright colours represented the cliff face and wide beach further down the coast at Treloose: this was one of his few recognisable paintings. Nicole hadn't been there since Connor left; she resolved to revisit as soon as she had some free time, so she could relive the day she and Connor had landed there from his boat, she wandering happily about while he set to work at his easel.

After listening to the ringing tone on the other end of the phone for a long time, she almost gave up — but then it stopped, and she heard Miss Burden's reedy tones announcing that this was the Melrose Gallery and how could she be of help?

Nicole cleared her throat, hardly

knowing how she could word her request for a contact number for Connor, but managing to get something out.

'I'm afraid it's not our policy to reveal telephone numbers to all and sundry.'

'But I'm not 'all and sundry',' said Nicole with spirit. 'I'm a friend of the artist from long ago wishing to contact him. Can you at least tell me the reason for the cancellation of the preview?'

Miss Burden's voice softened a little as she explained that it wasn't at all clear. Illness might have been the reason, but she didn't think so.

'I have some work of his I think he may have forgotten about,' said Nicole. 'I'd like the opportunity to ask him about it.'

In the silence that followed, she imagined the purple fingernails being examined as their owner contemplated the imagined enormity of what she was about to suggest.

'You may leave your telephone

number with me if you wish, and I'll see what I can do for you,' she said at last.

And with that, Nicole had to be content.

\*　\*　\*

She had forgotten that the steepness of the cliffs at Treloose meant visiting the beach down below was almost impossible — except from the sea. That was why it was such a private place, of course, and why they had had it to themselves for the time they were there.

It was she who had first shown it to Connor, peering down over the cliff edge from above. He had teased her by pretending to overbalance, and then laughed at her shrieks of alarm before pulling her to him in a warm hug. Even then, knowing how close to the edge they were, she couldn't relax and tried to pull away.

'Don't you trust me?' he had murmured into her hair.

She tried to shake the memory away as she stood on the cliff top now, listening to the pleasant hum of the sea down below. Behind her was the village of Treloose, but no sound came from the cottages, though there was some distant music from the pub on the corner. It was foolish to think of the Connor of long ago, and to imagine that the sounds she now heard — of someone climbing up the path from the beach — could be him. He had never done that as far as she knew, because the path seemed to come straight up the cliff and was so steep few people attempted it. Once, though, when they had landed on the beach at high tide, Connor had pretended that the water would come higher yet and they might have to scramble to the top.

'Carrying the boat with us?' she had said, laughing at him.

'Ah yes, the boat. I'd forgotten the boat.'

Connor had wanted to sketch the beach during this phase of the tide, when the breakers curled over the higher rocks at the end of the small cove, the sky behind them primrose-yellow and the palest pink. It was beautiful. Never to be forgotten. The painting she had shown Mary and Ken was the result of that one special evening.

As she watched, the gorse bushes parted and Daniel appeared, rather red of face from the climb. He paused, breathing heavily, and she saw he was carrying a hessian sack bulging with a knobbly cargo.

He stopped in surprise at seeing her.

'Hi there, Nicole, What brings you here?'

'I'd forgotten you lived in Treloose,' she said.

His lips twitched. 'Your social life not coming up to expectations?'

'My social life took a downturn before it even happened,' she said. 'Cancelled, would you believe? The preview of an art exhibition in Truro yesterday evening. I was looking forward to it.'

'At the Melrose Gallery?'

'That's the one.'

'Minna didn't tell me that.'

'Any reason why she should?'

'She works there sometimes, that's why.'

'Oh.'

He moved his cargo from one shoulder to the other.

'She invited me along, but I had work to do. Just as well, as it turns out, or it would have been a wasted evening for me too.'

'Mine wasn't entirely wasted,' Nicole said. 'A pleasant drive to Truro and back, a bit of socialising with neighbours, a booking for my B&B. Not a bad evening's work in the circumstances, wouldn't you say?'

'And a visit to Treloose now to round things off nicely.'

He was laughing at her and she wasn't sure she liked it. She almost said that she had a special reason for coming here. But how important was it really? The past was the past.

She tried to smile but knew she

wasn't making a good job of it.

Daniel seemed to think so too. 'Regrets?' he said sympathetically.

'For being here? For coming to live in Polvanion? Hardly. A beautiful place, everyone says.'

'Not all the time.'

'How do you mean?'

'Sad things happen. Disappointments, delayed hopes, loneliness. You name it. Just like everywhere else.'

'So being in a beautiful place doesn't help?'

'It's what's inside ourselves that matters, and we carry that with us.'

'What if we try to go back into the past, try to understand it better, and then move on?'

He shrugged. 'This is getting too deep for me.'

'I used to know Polvanion when I was young. I spent holidays here with my grandparents.'

'They lived here?'

'I did, too, for a couple of years.'

'So when would that have been?'

'I left ten years ago.'

'And you've never been back?'

She shook her head, remembering the suddenness of the decision for her to go to Bristol — her own or Grandpop's? Both, probably. It had all been so traumatic at the time that it was hard to remember. There had been Gran's diagnosis and illness and, when she died, Grandpop moving north to live with Uncle Jamie, and then dying too soon after. And all the time, Christa had been there for her.

'It didn't work out,' she said.

'I was in Australia then,' Daniel said. 'I moved back with my family in time to go to university. And there's a long, sad story, because I soon realised my mistake.' He smiled suddenly. 'How did we get onto such a gloomy subject? Fancy coming to my place over there and seeing what I do with this load of driftwood?'

She eyed his sack. 'So that's what it is?'

'I keep a store of it down below and

then collect what I need when I need it. A bit of a climb up but it's somewhere to keep it. There's a craft fair near Bodmin coming up soon and I'm working towards that.'

'It sounds intriguing.'

'Then come this way and I'll show you.'

She hesitated for only a moment.

Daniel's home was at the end of a row of terraced cottages, and at the side of the building was a lean-to shed with a door at either end. He had fixed up shelves around two walls, and on them were arranged a variety of objects that at first glance looked like a mass of abstract shapes.

He picked up one of them and handed it to her. 'My latest creation.'

She took it from him carefully, and could see now that what had once been a misshapen piece of sea-washed wood was now crafted into a group of sea shells on a flat surface obviously representing a beach. There were seagulls made out of the twisted wood, too, plus fantastically shaped fish and round sea urchins. Some were painted in subtle sea-colours and others left as they were. Now that her eyes were accustomed to the sight, Nicole exclaimed over the beauty of it all.

'And you made all these?'

'There are more out at the back. I need a good stock for sale with the season just starting. It's partly how I make my living.'

His voice sounded regretful now and she could see why. The shed was obviously too small for his needs, but was the largest he could fit into the available space. The middle of the floor was filled with pieces of furniture, some really old and all of it decrepit.

He smiled as he saw her looking at it. 'These are ready for a bit of work. Commissions, mainly, but some I picked up at local sales and can let myself rip on. This one for example.'

He picked up the nearest piece, a small spindly-looking table that seemed fit only for the rubbish tip.

'It must have been beautiful once,' she said.

'And will be again.'

'You can actually renovate that?'

'Not in the same way. It's too far gone for that. But look at the lines of it, the way the legs splay out. I only choose to work on things I love and can gain inspiration from. I've just completed a similar piece for an elderly client from Truro. Mrs Landon is her name, a charming person. She's so interested in what I do. I've almost finished that chest of drawers over there for her.'

Nicole exclaimed at its subtle colours of pearly grey, edged with turquoise with a silver trim.

'She wants to see the table in due course.'

'Will she buy it?'

He shrugged. 'That's not the reason for showing it to her.'

'So what happens to them, then?'

'They sell, with luck. Here and there, when I can persuade people to give them a space in their outlets. Not easy.'

Now she felt awkward. There was an unvoiced issue hanging between them. The stone hut.

'Minna's dad, Eddy, stores some of them for me at his place a mile or two inland. That's where my latest work has gone. His larger unit was hired by your elusive friend for a solo exhibition, I understand, but then it was cancelled.'

Nicole felt herself flush. 'You mean Connor Delaney?'

'The very one. You might be able to throw some light on his whereabouts?'

'No . . . I . . . He's not a close friend.'

Daniel smiled.

Nicole, moving a little, brushed against a footstool covered in green markings.

'Oh, I didn't see . . . '

'No matter.'

He picked it up and looked at it critically.

'I found this at the back of the Shack. Goodness knows how long it's been there, years probably. I've promised to do it up for Minna, but I'm not inspired yet. It will come.'

Nicole smiled. 'Thanks for showing me all this.'

'You'll come again? Or you might like to come out with me in the boat? It's a good way to see a bit of the coastline you haven't seen before. I can show you some superb places, and there's a good place to eat I know right on the beach.'

He put the stool down again and looked in disgust at his slimy hands.

'Yuk.'

Smiling, she said her farewells, and left without replying.

# 8

It was only later that Nicole thought about Daniel's eagerness to see her again. At first she had been surprised at his friendliness and his invitation to see his work, but had then forgotten these in her interest in it, especially when she saw some of the results. His driftwood creations were really something, and she could imagine the tourists snapping them up as soon as they saw them. She must make sure to mention them to any B&B guests who might be interested in something that must surely be unique. She should have asked Daniel to tell her some of the outlets he used since he didn't have a place big enough for a showroom here.

He hadn't been exactly unfriendly before, but this time his eyes had brightened with surprising enthusiasm as he saw her standing there on the top of the cliff. He had been obviously glad to rest for a moment after staggering up with that heavy-looking sack over one shoulder, but it seemed he was also pleased to see her. Or had that merely been because of his need for bigger premises that he wished to emphasise?

At the time she hadn't needed much persuasion to visit his home. Well, not his home exactly, just the lean-to shed he used as his workroom.

Her mind dwelt on this more than once as she checked the bedroom she had got ready for Mary and Ken's friends next day. When she had done all that was needed, she crossed to the window and gazed down on the stone hut across the lane. It was in such a perfect position. It was easily accessible; not far from the harbour, so that visitors to Polvanion could pick it out and make their way to it easily, perhaps to linger a while with the lovely view across the bay to enjoy. Placing seats outside on the grassy bank would be feasible, too, for customers to sit and view it.

But she couldn't quite dismiss the suspicion that Daniel's need for new premises was the only reason behind wanting to see her again. The feeling of being used was not a good one.

*   *   *

She turned away from the window as she heard the sound of a car engine outside, voices, and then the ring at her door bell.

Her first B&B guests had arrived!

The friends were younger than she had imagined, but obviously fond of Mary and Ken, who introduced them as Louise and Jem Shanklin and then withdrew.

Nicole, flushed with pleasure, showed them first the guests' dining- and sitting-room on the ground floor, and then their bedroom and the amenities upstairs.

Their appreciation was heart-warming.

'So we're your first guests, are we?' Jem said, smiling such a slow smile that it seemed to take forever to reach his eyes.

Louise, though, was bubbling over with enthusiasm. She rushed to the window, exclaiming at the view.

'Perfect. We'll be so happy here, Jem.'

'There's no reason why we shouldn't, my dear.'

'I'll leave you to unpack,' said Nicole. 'Just ask if there's anything you need.'

'Mary and Ken have loads of plans for us,' said Louise happily. 'Lunch in a place called the Shack to start with. What a name! I can't imagine what they've got lined up for us next, can you, Jem?' She giggled. 'A slaughter-house, perhaps, or a visit to the local gaol.'

Jem looked fondly at his wife. 'Take no notice of her. She gets like this sometimes. Totally mad.'

Nicole smiled as she went downstairs. If all her guests were as pleasant and as easily pleased with their accommodation as these two, she had nothing to fear. Louise reminded her a little of Christa, even though Louise was far more gushing and exuberant.

Maybe it was her silky fair hair and delicate build, and the way she had of looking at you with a quirky smile on her lips. Something, anyway, some hint that her sympathy was easily aroused.

She would never forget Christa's loving help. She had been kind from the first, doing all she could to make her home in Bristol a happy one for Nicole — which, over time, it became. Annette's down-to-earth good humour had helped too. Confiding in Christa had been easy and she had been the only one who knew exactly what had occurred with Connor. She had even hinted that something of the same sort had happened to herself once, and they were in this together.

So Nicole had owed Christa a great deal. And, of course, it was because of her legacy that she was here in Polvanion now. The stone hut seemed a fitting place as a memorial to her. She could never part with it.

★ ★ ★

Connor's phone call came on the following day when she was least expecting it. Louise and Jem had left after an early breakfast that Louise said was the best she had ever tasted in her life. Jem, his eyes raised to the ceiling in mock despair, had sighed.

'She says that every time. But this time, I must admit, she may have a point.'

'Of course I've got a point,' Louise said, laughing. 'Haven't I always?'

As soon as they had gone Nicole went upstairs and had just finished making the bed when the phone rang.

She ran lightly downstairs, hoping it was another booking.

'Hello. Cornerstone, Polvanion.'

'Nicole?'

The slightly husky voice sounded familiar, but at first she couldn't place it.

'Connor here. Connor Delaney. Is that really you, Nicole, my little friend of long ago?'

'Ten years,' she breathed.

'So long?'

She cleared her throat. 'Hello Connor. Thanks for phoning. I was disappointed not to see you the other evening.'

'Not as much as I was over not seeing you. They gave me your number. This is miraculous. You're still here and not flown away after all?'

'I came back,' she said. 'I live here now. Do you remember the stone hut?'

'Could I ever forget?' His voice was warm.

'I've been clearing the place out and several of your paintings turned up. I thought you might like them back.'

'My paintings, eh? Who would have thought it?'

'I took them with me to the preview to give them to you.'

'Ah, yes, the preview.'

There was silence for a moment.

Then he said, 'It would be good to see them again. Several canvases, you say? How would it be if I called in sometime to take a look?

'That sounds good, Connor.'

'That's settled then.'

'Where are you staying?'

Another silence.

Feeling awkward for having asked, Nicole ran her hand along the top of the bookcase in the passage, and then examined it for invisible dust. 'So when were you thinking of coming?' she asked.

'Well, yes, let me see now. This afternoon any good?'

'Why not? It will be good to see you again.'

'Fair enough. I'll be there.'

He rang off.

Nicole found it hard to settle to anything for the rest of the morning, and at last she gave up, made a mug of coffee and carried it across to the stone hut to drink it there. She propped the door and forced open the window to allow some fresh air to circulate. The place looked so much better now after the clear-out, and the daily airing had got rid of the musty smell. She had given the cord carpet a much-needed clean as well, and was surprised how good it looked. Two wooden chairs had remained, and a low stool, which she now hooked forward with one foot to sit on. From here, she had a good view across the ruffled water of the bay, and wondered if Connor had a place to stay where he could look out over the sea as he had once loved to do.

She sipped her coffee. It seemed surreal that he should be coming here this afternoon when she had hardly thought of him for years. At first, when she moved to Bristol, there had been deep hurt at the thought of never seeing him again. Going away from Polvanion was partly her own decision because the village would be empty without him, but Gran had thought it best, and so did Grandpop after a while. Perhaps he had regretted his harshness in sending Connor away, but that was something she would never know.

She had hidden her anguish from Christa as much as possible, but one night, after lying sleepless for hours, she had got up and crept downstairs and sobbed her heart out on the deep old-fashioned sofa in the study. And Christa had found her there.

Nicole finished her coffee and put the empty mug on the floor beside her. Keeping the paintings when she suspected their probable value would be dishonest. But Annette would be scathing about her getting in touch with Connor again, and no amount of explanation would wash with her. She would accuse her of ruses to get back together with him, but nothing was further from the truth. How could it be otherwise, after all this time?

The five canvases were lined up against the far wall where the light from the window showed them to the best advantage. It would take only a moment for Connor to decide whether or not he wanted them, and he was welcome to carry them off immediately. They were his, after all.

She stood up and moved closer. It was interesting how the light reflected back from them and highlighted certain things she might not have noticed otherwise. That rock on the first canvas, for instance. She could swear that the water had not long receded from it because of the shine at the base. It really was good. All of them would grace any exhibition, and one in particular — the painting she had taken over to the cottage for the night, which Mary had admired. She wondered that they had lain forgotten all these years, and that it hadn't been until Sophie had helped her with the clear-out that they had come to light. She hardly remembered them herself, and Connor clearly hadn't given them much thought.

At last she picked up her empty mug. Time to think of lunch so she could be ready for Connor's arrival.

★   ★   ★

Nicole jumped as the doorbell rang. She had just come in from the back garden with a basketful of dry washing, and was busy folding the items at the kitchen table. Because it was late in the afternoon, she had almost given up on Connor; but now she took a deep breath, walked slowly to the front door, and opened it.

Outside stood the girl, Minna, whom she had last seen serving pasties at the Shack on the day she had come to measure up for curtains and had met Daniel for the first time.

'Oh!'

'You're surprised to see me?' Minna's tone was curt.

'Well, yes, I was expecting . . . '

'Daniel?'

'Why should I be expecting Daniel?'

'No reason at all, if you've got any sense.'

'I don't understand.'

Minna glared at her. Nicole's first intention had been to invite her inside, but then she thought better of it. She felt at a distinct disadvantage but was determined to hold her own, even though she couldn't imagine what all this was about.

'I don't see what that has to do with

anything,' she said. 'I think you'd better explain and tell me why you are here.'

Minna took a step back and looked up at the wall where Tim had fixed the bracket ready for the B&B sign that would go up in due course.

'You soon got that up in place. Where else are you advertising?'

For a moment Nicole didn't reply. This was a distinctly odd conversation and there seemed to be a subtext she couldn't quite work out.

'You'll have to tell me why you need to know,' she said at last.

'Some of your so-called B&B clients were at the Shack today.'

'Yes, having lunch. They said that was where they were going. They didn't misbehave, I hope, and start throwing pasties about?'

Frowning, Minna ignored that. There were obviously far more serious things to consider.

'They were full of this place. Said how nice you'd got it, how well-looked-after they felt themselves to be, and

117

how lucky they were to be here.'

A flush of pleasure swept through Nicole at this unexpected praise. She smiled. 'They're kind people, that's why.'

'Or they've been bribed.'

'That's insulting.'

'They're not just guests, are they? Not people you know, just staying with you for a holiday?'

Taken aback at her effrontery, Nicole waited.

'I can see they're not,' Minna said. 'It's written all over your face. They're the paying public.'

'What if they are? This is my business and mine only. I'm not answerable to you or anyone else. I think you had better go.'

'Oh, I think you *are* answerable.'

Nicole made a move to close the door but Minna was too quick for her.

'Not so fast!'

Since her foot was wedged in the doorway, Nicole had no choice. She eyed the telephone on the hall table, too far away to reach.

Minna's expression was ugly.

'I shall report you to the council and see what they have to say about it. That is, unless . . . '

'Unless what?'

'Unless you promise to leave Daniel alone.'

Nicole gazed at her, astonished. She was unable to think of a fitting response before Minna spun around on her heel and was gone. She was talking non-sense. Everything was above-board, and soon there would be all the certificates she needed to prove her fitness for running such an establishment. She was waiting for them before hanging the board in position, but there was nothing to stop her from taking guests at once. Minna must have known that, and her obvious dislike of Nicole as a newcomer was daunting. It seemed likely that she was the person respon-sible for cancelling the carpet-fitter's visit. She should have thought of that and confronted the girl to see what she had to say. Too late now.

Nicole slammed shut the door, and stood leaning on it for a few moments to regain her composure. Being detested to such a degree was horrible. She was still trembling a little when the telephone rang.

She sprang to answer it. This time she recognised Connor's deep voice.

'Something's come up,' he said. 'I'll be involved till about six. Or seven, maybe even later. What do you say to me getting to you around eight or so? We can get a bite to eat somewhere and do some catching-up. How does that sound?'

'Well . . .'

'Good. I'll see you then. Put some glad rags on.'

'Yes, well . . .'

He rang off. Nicole looked at the receiver in her hand as if she hardly knew what it was, then put it down carefully. He hadn't mentioned the paintings, the reason for his visit, so what was going on? Too late to ask him now. He seemed to have definite ideas of his own. Was this going to be her life from now on, being pushed around by others? Only if she let it, and she wasn't about to do that. She thought of Louise and Jem's good-humoured appreciation, and Sophie Penberthy's willingness to help. Mary and Ken next door, too, were pleased to recommend her place to their friends. So she wouldn't let one crazy girl and an unreliable man, for whom she was only trying to do a good and honest thing, run her life. She was going to make a few decisions of her own. And the first of these was to make a strong mug of coffee and, while drinking it, decide what she was going to do to fill in the next few hours.

# 9

The breeze died away, and the early evening was one of those calm ones where the water in the harbour at high tide was silky-smooth and unruffled by even the slightest movement — until Nicole set off with Daniel in his boat. Not a vessel at anchor shifted, and only the wake as they headed out to the open sea left a clear line of progress behind them.

'Where has all the wind gone?' she said.

At the tiller, Daniel looked across at her and smiled.

'It's not all strong winds here and waves and surf crashing against the cliffs,' he said.

She laughed. 'Heat waves sometimes? Temperatures soaring, thunderstorms, hail, gale-force winds . . . '

'Changeable, anyway.'

'But we're lucky this evening.'

'So we are. And that's why it's the ideal time to collect the rest of my wood,' he said.

Nicole was seated in the bows, and she leaned over a little to exclaim on the clearness of the water as they veered to the right, following the coastline to Treloose. When she looked up again, she could see the stone hut, and beyond that the row of cottages where she had been just a short time ago.

Earlier, she had placed on her bed a selection of her clothes she hoped would pass as glad rags, ready for a last-minute decision when it was time for her to get ready for Connor's visit. Then, that done, she had decided on a walk — not only for fresh air to blow away some of the annoyance left by Minna's visit, but also to remind herself that Polvanion was her home now, and no one was going to dictate to her how to live her life.

She had calmed down a little before she met Daniel on his way to his boat, and had readily agreed to accompany him to collect his stack of driftwood from the beach at Treloose to bring back to store behind the Shack.

She had happy memories of Connor taking her there that long-ago summer, and here was the chance to go there again. There was plenty of time.

Daniel's face lit up. 'You will? It won't take long but it's a job that needs doing.'

And a pleasant one at that, Nicole thought now, trailing her hand in the water. She lifted it out and watched the drops trickle into the tranquil sea.

'So why are you taking the wood to the Shack?' she said.

'It was Eddy's suggestion. He likes to help where he can. That's Minna's dad, a kind man.'

Unlike his daughter, she thought. Unlike herself, as well, now she came to think of it. The stone hut was there, empty of everything except a couple of old chairs. And Connor's paintings, of course, but they would soon be gone.

From Daniel's point of view, the stone hut was perfect for his needs. She wondered that he didn't mention it. He looked perfectly content as he sat at the tiller with the evening sun on his face.

Daniel glanced at her. 'Why so serious?'

'Thinking, that's all.'

'Not pleasant thoughts?'

'Much better now.' She smiled suddenly, knowing it was true. It felt good to know that Daniel had been pleased to see her; he'd welcomed her aboard with such calm pleasure, as if it was the most natural thing in the world to have her company and he wasn't thinking of the stone hut at all.

'Eddy's always been interested in what I'm doing,' he said. 'He's hot on encouragement, that man, and I needed encouragement when I gave up on university some years ago and came back to Cornwall to set up this odd way of earning my living.'

'To a lot of disapproval?'

He shrugged.

'You could say that. All forgotten now though.'

'So you gave up a place at university?' She couldn't help the surprise in her voice. It was hard to imagine Daniel giving up on anything. He seemed the dogged type, quietly getting on with life and making the best of things.

'I was studying law, my father's profession. But I soon realised it wasn't for me. I should have realised that before and saved a lot of trouble.'

'Hindsight's a fine thing,' she said. 'We can't always know at the time what we really want, but it needs courage to make such a life change.'

'Or desperation. All in the past now.'

'But don't you think the past is always with us because it's made us what we are?' she said.

He smiled. 'It's the future that counts on an evening like this.'

'Not the present?'

'That too,' he conceded. 'It's all we have really, isn't it, the present?'

'It's beautiful here, Daniel,' she said.

She felt that his words were true, but she was still finding it hard to relax after what Minna had demanded. 'Can I ask you something — it's all right to start up a B&B without getting special permission from the council first, isn't it?'

'I don't see why not.'

'I'm getting everything in place I think I need to do.'

'But you're worried you've missed something?'

'A bit.'

'Then you shouldn't be. I'll check it out for you to make quite certain, if you like. But I'm sure there's no need to worry. I'll let you know at once if there is.'

'Thank you.'

He looked so full of assurance, sitting there looking at her in concern, that she felt light-hearted now, and able to enjoy her surroundings to the full.

Ahead of them was the line of sand that meant they had almost arrived. Daniel said nothing more as he cut the engine and they glided in to shore. When they were close, he swung his legs over the side, and Nicole rolled up the legs of her jeans, wishing she were wearing shorts too.

'Stay where you are for a moment,' he said. 'No need for you to get wet.'

The boat shuddered as it touched the sand.

'Now!'

His hand felt warm and encouraging as he helped her out onto dry land. Together they pulled the boat clear of the water. Daniel checked that it was high enough above the tide-line and then stood up straight and stretched.

Nicole gazed in awe at the towering cliffs.

'Look at the height of those. No wonder it's almost impossible to get up there from the beach, especially carrying a huge load. But you did it the other evening.'

'Needs must. I wanted some pieces urgently at the time, and couldn't wait to collect them by boat.'

'I see.'

And she did, of course. He had shown her his tiny workshop that was far too small for storing much in the way of material. She wished she hadn't commented.

She looked up at the cliffs again, marvelling that they were as high as she remembered. Two days after she'd pointed out the beach to him, Connor had brought her here — along with his painting gear — and she had spent a long, happy time watching him at work.

She shook the memory away as Daniel indicated she should come with him across the sand to the rocks at the end of the beach. When they got there, she saw that between them and the cliff was a perfect hiding place for the various shapes of driftwood he had collected. The sea here was dotted with submerged rocks, and she could see that it would be dangerous to get nearer by boat.

Daniel picked up an armful of wood and Nicole did the same.

'This lot would be quite safe here until the next extra-high tide,' he said. 'That's not due for the next week or two, but Eddy thinks it's best to move it now. I'm only too pleased to take advantage of his offer. He'll store it under cover for me, and that's useful.'

She looked at him quickly and saw that his expression was calm and pleasant. There was no bitterness there, no hint that she could have provided storage space in a far more convenient place.

'Come on, then, let's go,' he said.

There was more wood than Nicole had thought at first, and by the time the boat was loaded she thought there might not be room for her as well.

'Don't worry, I won't leave you behind,' Daniel said, smiling.

They didn't speak much on the way back, but there was a feeling of companionship between them that felt right. She was sorry when Polvanion was in sight again as they rounded the headland. Daniel slowed the engine as though he too felt the same.

There were a few people around the harbour area now, visitors perhaps, enjoying the lovely evening. She didn't recognise anybody as they continued on their way to the beach of Penvenna.

Nicole knew the drill now: wait in the boat until it touched dry land. Daniel helped her out.

'Now for a bit more work,' he said.

She smiled. 'Lead on.'

It was harder this time because they had to carry the wood up the narrow path to the Shack. There was a small lean-to shed here, open to the elements, but providing sufficient shelter for Daniel's purposes. A stack of driftwood was already there, and he looked at it in approval.

'Minna's been busy on my behalf,' he said. 'She's a good girl.'

Nicole said nothing.

'Have I tired you out?'

She hastened to reassure him. 'No, no, not a bit. I've enjoyed it, Daniel. Really.'

She had hoped Minna would be here to see them, but that was an unworthy thought and she was ashamed of it now. Daniel was a pleasant companion and she had been glad to help, that was all. She had no wish to spoil any friendship between him and Minna, and she would have indicated that if Minna hadn't been so confrontational.

Back in the boat again, they were soon once more in the harbour. Daniel helped Nicole up the steps in the wall. For a moment, she felt his hand tighten on hers. Then, smiling, he let her go.

'Another time,' he said, his voice low.

She felt herself flush, aware now of a magic in the air that seemed to lift her away from everyday Polvanion. The beauty of the evening had got to her at last, that and the feeling of freedom from being on the water away from shore.

That was all.

★  ★  ★

Dusk was beginning to fall when at last a car draw up outside, and Nicole knew that Connor was finally here. She felt strangely calm as she went downstairs to greet him.

'Nicole!'

His voice had the warm timbre she remembered, but the man standing there seemed at first glance to be a complete stranger. His long flowing hair, now greying a little at the temples, had been tamed into a short, neat style, and his dark suit made him look taller than she remembered.

He held out both hands.

'Let me look at you!'

Flushing a little under his scrutiny, she smiled.

'Will I do?'

'Wonderfully, my dear. How good it is to meet again. But how has tomboy Nicole turned into such a beautiful woman, tell me that?'

She was confused. 'Tomboy?'

'A wild and lovely girl, as I remember.'

That was better.

He looked rueful, and for a moment seemed suddenly to lose the years between now and then.

'And I'm late again, but no matter. They know me well.'

'So where are we going?'

He looked mysterious as he beckoned her to follow him to the car. It wasn't until they were speeding along the narrow lanes out of the village that Nicole remembered the paintings he had come to collect. But they appeared to be the last things on Connor's mind, and when she mentioned them, he shrugged his broad shoulders and gave the secret smile that she had found so attractive long ago.

'Time enough to think of them, my dear, time enough.'

She felt awkward suddenly, not sure of why she was here.

'I wondered, that's all.'

He flicked a sideways glance at her.

'Worry not, my little one. Tomorrow is another day. Or the day after. They won't run away.'

'You're not curious about them?'

'Mere daubs, no doubt, done in my youth and then forgotten.'

His tone of utter disregard was hurtful. But he seemed to pick up on her reaction because his voice softened a little as they reached the main road and waited for a van to pass. He patted her hand.

'A figure of speech, my dear. Modesty, if you like. As I remember, there's no artificial lighting in the building, and it will soon be dark. Daylight would be best to view them.'

'Well, yes.' She hadn't thought of that.

'Well, then.'

They turned right again now and Connor drove confidently down the high-banked lane. She knew now where they were going because this was the only way down by road to the beach and the Penvenna Hotel.

'So you're staying at the hotel?' she said.

'And there's a table booked for us with a superior view, just in case. It was that or a picnic on the beach.'

She laughed. But 'just in case' of what — that she would meet with his approval when she answered the door to him? So, she had passed a test; it felt good.

'Or a pasty at the Shack,' she said.

'The Shack?'

'A wooden building, up behind the beach and hidden from it, where they serve snacks. It's very popular.'

'But not for the likes of us.' He sounded complacent, as well he might be if he could afford to stay in such a prestigious hotel. She thought of Daniel and his stacks of driftwood she had helped him store at the Shack only a short time before.

'Pensive again, my dear?'

'A little tired, I think.'

'And hungry?'

She smiled. 'That too.'

It felt good being hustled into the warmth of the hotel's comfortable dining room and being shown to the table in the window. The subtle scent from the lilies in the fireplace floated across to them, and the murmur of conversation around them was pleasant.

The waiter pulled out a chair for her and placed her napkin on her lap. Then he handed her the menu. She smiled her thanks.

Connor leaned back in his chair as he perused the menu, and the overhead light burnished his dark hair and highlighted the deepness of the lines from nose to mouth. It was a strong face, Nicole thought; more rugged now than in his youth, but attractive all the same. His air of self-confidence was, too, and she noticed one or two of the women diners glancing his way.

There was red snapper with coriander and Puy lentils on the menu, and a starter of watercress and celeriac soup that seemed to Nicole to complement it well. Connor made a swift choice too, and in no time the wine waiter was at their table.

Connor's forehead creased in concentration as he took some moments to choose a Pinot Noir and then a claret. That done, he leaned back in his chair and gave a sigh of contentment.

'It feels like a celebratory meal,' Nicole said.

'And why not?' His eyes glittered at her.

Her cheeks felt warm. Years ago, her grandfather had sent Connor away from the place where he was establishing himself as a significant artist. It was she who should be making amends to him now. Returning some forgotten paintings to him that might or might not be of value was nothing compared with the luxury of this.

She glanced around. The room, with its wide windows overlooking the headland and the darkening sea, looked as if it had been furnished in Victorian times by someone of the utmost good taste. Even the ceiling was delicately decorated in white carvings of flowers and birds. The small chandelier in the centre glittered with a soft light on the silken threads in the crimson curtains looped back from the windows.

As they ate, they talked of many things, and Connor's interest in her life in Bristol was flattering. Then he told her of his travels around the world, exhibiting his work wherever he could — until a collector befriended him, and he was on his way up.

'The rest is history,' he said.

They both chose hot chocolate soufflé with chocolate sauce for their dessert, followed by a selection of biscuits and cheese for Connor. They drank their coffee as the last diners were leaving, and Nicole stood up to go at last with a feeling of regret.

In the vestibule, Connor caught hold of her elbow and nodded to the receptionist.

Nicole glanced at her and froze.

Minna?

But Minna, flushing a little, was looking directly at Connor. He acknowledged her interest with a slight bow and then turned to Nicole.

'Would you care to come upstairs?' he murmured.

She hadn't known his intention of coming here to the Penvenna Hotel when he had phoned earlier, supposing him to be anxious only to view his paintings in the stone hut and then going somewhere modest to eat. She had been naive.

In the few seconds that this spun through her head, she saw that Minna was looking confused. As well she might, Nicole thought.

She smiled at Connor.

'It's been a wonderful evening, Connor, but no,' she said, struggling to sound apologetic. 'I have to be up early in the morning, you see, slaving away at the stove. You do understand?'

'Of course,' he said smoothly. 'Then shall we go?'

Nicole was aware of Minna's eyes boring into her back as Connor helped her on with her jacket and then held open the door for her. The evening air felt cool on her cheeks and she shivered a little.

'I'm afraid I embarrassed you,' he said.

'Not at all. Please . . . '

'But we'll meet again, of course.' A statement rather than a question.

'Of course. There are your paintings in the stone hut. We mustn't forget them.'

He laughed. 'No, indeed.'

The atmosphere between them felt lighter again now, and over on the horizon a huge moon appeared. Nicole drew in a breath of pure pleasure at the silvery glimmers on the sea.

'I shall paint that,' he said.

'It will make a beautiful picture.'

'And you shall be the first to see it.'

Even Minna was forgotten in her glow of gratification at this promise. All of a sudden, she wanted to express her gratitude for the meal he had given her in such beautiful surroundings, but all she could think of was to talk of his lost canvasses and to tell him what an impact they had had on her when they were discovered.

'It was like finding buried treasure,' she said,

'Hardly that.'

'Had you really forgotten such exciting work?'

He was silent for so long that she thought she had offended him.

'Well, no,' he said at last. 'Not if I'm really honest. Occasionally through the years they've come to mind.'

They reached the car and he opened her door for her. As she got in she smiled up at him.

'I hope you are not disappointed when you see them, Connor.'

'I don't think that's possible,' he said quietly as he got in and turned the key in the ignition.

His simple words seemed to imply something more, and again she felt the same awkwardness she had experienced when she opened her door to him earlier. To fill a silence that seemed heavy with meaning, she tried to concentrate on making arrangements for him to view his work some other time.

'Let me see. What's the best I can do? In a day or two, I think,' he said.

She had hoped for the following day, but perhaps that was expecting too much. She knew he was in the area to sort out the details of his postponed exhibition in the Melrose Gallery. He would have work to do in connection with that.

They were driving down through the village now, and she couldn't see the moon at the moment, only the glittering path across the water.

# 10

In his small front room of his Treloose cottage, Daniel looked critically at the renovated chest of drawers he had brought in from his workshop to allow room for his next project. He was due to deliver the chest tomorrow to his elderly friend who lived on the outskirts of Truro.

He had been attracted to the piece of furniture, and had agreed at once to take on the work, relieved that he didn't have to disappoint Mrs Landon. From the first, he had vowed to work only on pieces that spoke to him, and this one certainly did that. How long it had been up in her attic he didn't know, but it deserved some tender loving care because it was such a beautiful thing, and obviously made by loving hands many years ago. Although in a dreadful condition, its unique style appealed to him — and obviously had to her too when she discovered it in the family home. His advertisement in *The Cornish Guardian* had caught her attention, and she had called to ask about his services.

He had been surprised at her knowledge of Chalk Paint when she telephoned him to ask if he was interested in working on the chest, because not everyone knew of its unique qualities — or, for that matter, wanted their dilapidated furniture to have a new lease of life in this imaginative way. But Mrs Landon had plenty of imagination, and listened to his advice with her grey head tilted a little to one side and an air of interest that was flattering.

He had taken with him the colour chart from his workshop wall, and she had exclaimed in delight when he showed it to her and suggested the subtle colours he thought suitable. Between them they chose a delicate shade of grey with parts of the drawers picked out in pale turquoise edged with silver. He could see the finished effect in his mind's eye and was pleased with her ready agreement, hoping she could see it too. Many people couldn't, but most were brave enough to take his word for it.

'I like to collect the paint myself from the stockist I use up country,' he said. 'That way I can make sure it's the exact shade we had in mind.'

'And of course you'll wax it when it is done.'

He had laughed. 'I see you know as much about it as I do.'

'Not quite,' she had said, shrugging her slim shoulders. 'Not as much as I might sound. I'm interested in all the inventor of Chalk Paint has accomplished since she set up twenty or more years ago. I'm all for a bit of entrepreneuring, if that's a word. And now she has businesses all over the world. I like the sound of that.'

He did too, and said so. That was what he was doing, after all; believing in himself and following a dream without knowing if he would be successful or not.

He had got to know Mrs Landon

well when she had come to see how he was progressing with the job, and once he had taken her across to the Shack because she had said that pasties weren't what they were when she was a girl. It was great to prove her wrong.

Minna had been kind to her, and it was through Mrs Landon's connections that she had found the receptionist's job at the Melrose Gallery, filling in when needed, and the part-time work at the Penvenna Hotel.

Daniel whistled softly as he ran his hand over the smooth surface of the renovated chest, a tune remembered from his childhood. Now, what was it? The knowledge was nearly there, hovering at the back of his mind. Something haunting by Handel, a question. *Have you not seen my lady go down the garden singing? Blackbird and thrush and...* But that was all. An old-fashioned sort of song. It was strange that it had come to him when thinking of Mrs Landon and this chest of drawers that was anything but old-fashioned after the treatment he had given it.

He would be sorry to see it go.

\* \* \*

Nicole took pleasure in visiting the stone hut in her free moments during the next few days, imagining herself back in the past when she had first met Connor. Annette would tell her that she was on dangerous ground here, and that you could never relive the past because the intervening years changed you and everyone else. But, Nicole told herself, for some it might be exactly the right thing to do. You heard of couples reuniting after many years of losing touch; friends, too.

On Sunday morning it was another of those calm days she so enjoyed. While she was waiting for Connor's arranged arrival, she went across to the stone hut to gaze out across the bay to Chapel Head. A slight mist hovered and gave the bay that mysterious air she loved. The hut was like a calm refuge where she could come to refresh her spirits — and to remember Christa too, and the part she had unknowingly played in her new way of life.

Annette had phoned only that morning, wanting to know the latest developments with her B&B guests, and Nicole was able to tell her that they had been persuaded to stay on for the next week too, so she was well pleased. She neglected to tell Annette about her meeting with Connor, and she certainly didn't mention that he had taken her to dinner at the hotel. She knew what Annette's reaction to that would be, and smiled now as she thought of it.

They had talked instead of how helpful Sophie Penberthy had been, and how Nicole would like to offer her a job when her business really got going. There would be no time then for socialising and accepting invitations from anyone, and certainly not from Connor. But there had been no harm in having dinner with him on Wednesday evening. In fact, it might even have done her a bit of good if it resulted in Minna forgetting the threats she had made.

She glanced at the five canvases lined up against the far wall ready for their creator's examination. They seemed to exude as much personality as Connor himself, and she would miss them when they were taken away.

* * *

Even though he was early, it seemed natural to see him striding towards her from the direction of the harbour.

'I can't stay long,' he had said when he phoned last evening. 'Expect me late morning. I trust it's convenient for you?'

Very much so. And to have him come earlier was a bonus. She smiled a welcome.

'At last,' he said warmly as he reached her. He gave her a quick hug and a peck on the cheek

The door of the stone hut stood wide open, and Connor ducked his head to go through into the dim interior. He stood for a moment getting his bearings, his dark head almost touching the rafters.

'There's a different smell in here now,' he said.

'You remember what it was like after all these years?'

'Cord carpet; fairly new, I think. And apples. Burning ash from the stove. Turps, of course. Your perfume is different too, my dear. A light, flowery one then, more sophisticated now. Subtle. I like it.'

His eyes glowed at her and she felt a flicker of something she couldn't name. A revival of the feelings she had once had for him? She froze.

He seemed to notice nothing. She must say something to fill this intense silence.

'And now?'

He sniffed. 'Mmm. Nothing much. Cleanliness, perhaps. Emptiness, certainly. And now my eyes are getting accustomed to the gloom, I can see why. So much has been cleared away.'

'But not your paintings.'

'Ah, no. My early work. And this.' He picked up the conch shell that Nicole loved because of the memories it had for her. Christa had bought it in St Ives when they had visited it together years ago. She had laughed at the way she could hear the sea in it when she held it to her ear. She wanted Nicole to have it, and it lived on the narrow windowsill for the summer. She had made sure it went with her to Bristol, though, and now it was back here again.

'My godmother, Christa, bought it,' Nicole said.

Connor nodded and put it down again. He moved towards his paintings and stood gazing in silence.

She waited.

After a while, he let out a long breath. 'Not as bad as I feared. I would like to take one of them with me now for the forthcoming exhibition, as an example of my early work. They like to show progression, and most of mine have gone.'

'You kept none of it?'

'Eirys didn't. I came back from a trip one day and it had all vanished. And so had she. That's how it was, you see, just before I came here to Polvanion.'

'Eirys?'

He was silent for a long moment, his face sombre. 'My work, my precious work. All gone.'

Her heart was filled with sympathy for him.

'No need to look sad, my dear. Our relationship was going nowhere. It was for the best for both of us.' He picked up the painting and held it towards her.

'Of course you must take it,' she said. 'They're all yours.'

'I did it *in situ*, if you recall, at Chapel Head. Remember that cold, blustery day when the surf was lashing the cliff, and that young lad nearly overbalanced and his dad gave him a walloping?'

'I wasn't there,' Nicole said.

He looked at her in surprise. 'Were you not?'

'How do you know the man was his dad?'

'I was that man.'

'You?'

'Indeed me. Ryan deserved it, believe me.'

'You have a son?'

Connor shrugged. 'He's in the States with his mother now, I believe. It's the way it worked out. But a teenage boy needs his father. I'd have him with me, but I lead a wandering life.'

She could well imagine that. But Connor with a son he had never mentioned! She could hardly believe it. She was silent, wondering who had been with them on that windy day at Chapel Head. There was so much she didn't know about him.

'I felt compelled to stay painting in that place, in spite of the conditions,' Connor said. 'Or because of them, who knows?'

Nicole nodded. The painting that was the result interested her for the way he had dealt with the sea and the sky.

'And the rest of the work is yours,' he said, turning to her again with a broad smile. 'Keep them or destroy them as you will.'

'As if I would!'

He laughed. 'And now I must go.'

With the painting held under one arm, he lowered his head in the doorway as he followed her out. A man and a woman outside Cornerstone across the lane saw them, and waved apologetically to Nicole.

She waved back.

'My B&B guests,' she told him. 'Forgotten something, most likely. They went out soon after breakfast.'

'Is that so? For a moment I thought it was someone I knew; someone with that same honey-coloured hair, fine and silky. And good legs.'

For a moment Nicole was puzzled.

'She has the same smooth way of walking,' he said. 'It's uncanny.'

Light dawned and Nicole smiled.

'So you met my godmother, Christa?'

'I lived here, remember?'

Christa had been here on a visit to Polvanion during that summer, Nicole thought, so she shouldn't be surprised, even though Christa had never said that she had met Connor. So having the four remaining paintings of Connor's here in the stone hut would seem suitably fitting, because Christa might have seen him at work on them.

'So where is she now?' he said.

Nicole turned to put the key in the lock.

'I'm going to regard this place as a memorial to her,' she said quietly. 'She died, about a year ago.'

'I see.'

She felt comforted by his simple words, because it felt as if he understood how hard it still was to talk of her. Being back in Polvanion had brought home the deep loss she still felt. She had been thinking of Christa a lot lately, wishing she could have known that Nicole's home was here now and she was happy to be back.

'And you say you take B&B guests?

Now, that's really interesting.'

'I'm just starting up. It seemed a good way to make a living.'

Connor nodded. Then he took a step back and looked up at the slate roof of the building.

'There's some value in that,' he said.

'And the rest of it too,' she said, smiling now.

'Indeed.'

'Can I offer you a coffee or something before you go?'

'I don't think you're going to get rid of me so fast after all. I've suddenly had an idea or two to put to you.'

'Now, that sounds intriguing.'

'I'd like to sound you out on something, and it's a lovely day. What would you say to walking me part-way home, stopping off at that ramshackle old place behind the beach and having our coffee there? A good place to talk, I think.'

She thought swiftly of the ironing she had planned and of the overgrown garden at the back that needed urgent attention. But how could they compete against this suggestion of Connor's?

'I'd like that.'

His eyes twinkled at her. 'Then let's go.'

* * *

Connor's idea turned out to be more interesting than she could have imagined, and she had plenty to think about when they parted at last and she set out to walk back towards the harbour. His exhibition at the Melrose Gallery was to be staged in the autumn, and since he wanted to stay in the area until then, he had been asked to run a series of outside workshops during the summer on painting the sea. He was looking for a venue on the coast to act as a base.

'They've already had some enquiries from people up country,' he said, leaning both arms on the wooden table and gazing at Nicole earnestly. 'They pressed me to agree, but it's not so easy to find somewhere that can provide accommodation for the students at the same time.'

'The stone hut?' she said. 'Would there be enough space?'

'How would you feel about that? I thought of you at once, Nicole, and your needing the business. Two of them would be day students returning to their homes each night. You could provide overnight accommodation for four.'

'B&B?'

'And an evening meal. Each group will come a week at a time. Six nights. Four from upcountry and two local. How does it sound?'

'All through the summer, you said?'

'That's right.' He took a sip of coffee, found it was cooler than he had thought, and then downed the rest. 'Drink up or it will be cold.'

She did as he said. The place was busy but the chatter round them seemed surreal because of what Connor was suggesting. She saw that Sophie Penberthy was helping out, otherwise

Minna's father would have been on his own.

'So what about lunches?' she said.

'Those too, of course, for the four residents. Packed ones, I think, and the local people will bring their own. We'll be painting *en plein air* most days in the mornings — in the open air,' he clarified. 'Weather permitting, of course. The afternoons — back in the studio, working in their chosen medium. Oils mainly, I think.'

She thought of the stone hut being used just as it had once before, as an artist's studio. But this time there would be seven people there, dragging their easels as they jostled for space. The smell of the oils and thinning medium, cries of dismay as paint plopped in smelly globules on the cord flooring, and the scrape of palette knives as they tried to remove it.

It would mean that the stone hut would be virtually lost to her for the whole summer, but did that matter? She would see Connor every day.

Connor had no doubt that the workshops would be popular, and said so with confidence that made his eyes shine. He placed his hand on hers and patted it. The warmth from it was encouraging.

'Poor little Nicole! I've dropped this on you too suddenly, haven't I?' he said. 'We'd need a firm booking for six weeks at least. It needs thinking about. Why not sleep on it and let me know tomorrow? How does that sound?'

The feel of his hand on hers was almost enough for her to make a snap decision, but she must be absolutely sure it was what she wanted.

'Here tomorrow at the same time?' he said.

She smiled. 'Here tomorrow, Connor. And I promise to think about it.'

'Good girl,' he said as he got to his feet.

She basked in his approval as they walked the short way down to the beach, and they parted.

# 11

As if she could think of anything else! The ironing was done with her hardly realising it, but as she began some half-hearted weeding of the flower bed at the back, she found she was wasting her time. She would be better employed in getting some lunch for herself, and then going right away from here for a while, somewhere she could think Connor's plan through with no distractions. Chapel Head? Why not?

She could hardly believe that this was her first visit because the rocky headland seemed so familiar. This was, of course, because some of the paintings Connor had left behind featured this area. When she had looked at them, she had almost felt the breeze on her face and the rocky terrain beneath her feet because of the vibrant colours he had used to portray the scene as he saw it.

Now, as she parked and set out to walk to the end of the headland, she was feeling it for real.

The sparse turf was dotted here and there with clumps of foliage and the occasional late cowslip that had been reluctant to brave the spring winds — probably fiercer up here on the exposed headland. She saw late violets, too. Above her, larks trilled, and there was a flurry of seagulls a little way offshore. She saw a fishing boat churning through messy seas further out, and with the breeze came a faint fishy smell that pleased her as she stood there at the end of the land.

She stayed there for some minutes and then, looking round, saw a smooth rock in an indent in the land that provided not only shelter, but privacy too, just in case anyone else was foolhardy enough to venture this far on a breezy Sunday afternoon. From here she looked across the bay to Polvanion in the far distance: too far away to pick out any distinguishing marks.

She thought of the stone hut over there. Restoring it to a peaceful place for relaxation had been her objective almost as soon as she had seen it again. And then she had thought of Christa, and the idea of a memorial to her had seemed a good one. But so was Connor's plan of renting it for the summer for use as a studio base for his workshops. A temporary base only, she reminded herself. In the autumn he would be gone, and it would become again the peaceful place she had planned. But there was the whole summer before her and it was promising to be the best one of her life.

Connor's plan would benefit her B&B business because it would ensure that Cornerstone was fully-booked throughout the season. No need to concentrate on ways to publicise it by expensive advertisements and the like. She could cope with the evening meals and the packed lunches too. It would be financially worthwhile. Annette would be pleased with her for not hankering after the past, but concentrating on the present and future. And so would Tim, in his quiet way. And she would see more of Connor.

So, a win-win situation. Yes, most definitely.

She leapt up, anxious now to get home and start making a list of things to be done. And another of questions to ask Connor when she saw him tomorrow morning.

★  ★  ★

Penvenna beach was deserted the next day when Nicole arrived. She stood for a moment looking out across the beach to the grey sea and Chapel Head in the bleak distance. Most people would have other plans on such a disappointing Sunday morning, and she was surprised to find the Shack open for business.

Minna was there wiping down the worktop with her back to her. She turned as Nicole approached.

'Coffee?' Minna's voice was subdued. 'It's on the house.'

'Sorry?'

'You heard.'

'I thought that's what you said.'

'Milk, no sugar?'

'Thank you.'

Perplexed, Nicole seated herself where she could see the end of the slipway to watch for Connor's arrival. When Minna came with the coffee she looked pale and hesitant.

'He's round those rocks, painting,' she said abruptly. 'I wasn't going to tell you.'

Nicole slid the mug towards her. 'Why not?'

'I was out of order the other day, making that phone call to cancel the fitter. I don't know what got into me. I don't mean it, not now.' She swiped at an insect that dared to encroach. 'Dad said to apologise, so I have.'

She had apologised in a sort of way, Nicole thought, and it would do. She smiled. 'It doesn't matter, Minna. The man came in the end and made a good job of it. Think no more about it. I

166

don't.' She was relieved at the outcome, though. Unpleasantness in any form was not good, especially in a small place like Polvanion. She felt touched, too, by Minna's clumsy efforts to put things right.

'You're not busy at the moment,' she said. 'Why don't you get a drink for yourself and join me?'

Minna face lit up. 'Connor will be back soon,' she said. 'I was supposed to tell you that, too.'

Instead of coffee Minna brought a glass of water and sat at the picnic table opposite Nicole to drink it. She still seemed uneasy, pushing imaginary strands of hair away from her face and looking repeatedly towards the rocks at the base of the cliff.

'Have you got lots of bookings yet?' she said abruptly.

Nicole looked at her, not smiling this time. Minna's silly threat had worried her at the time — not because she believed it would have any effect, but because of the ill-feeling behind it.

'I didn't phone the council,' said Minna.

'No. But it was a stupid idea, wasn't it?'

'Dad said.'

'A sensible man, your dad.'

'So that's all right then?'

'Well, yes. That's all right — if you're really regretting it?'

Minna nodded and took a sip of water. Then she looked longingly in the direction of the rocks. 'I wish I could go to one of Connor's classes.'

Nicole was surprised. 'You know about them?'

'Only what I overheard. Connor was telling Mrs Landon about it last night.'

'Mrs Landon was at the hotel?'

'Of course she was.' Minna's smile was radiant now. 'Look, Connor's coming back.'

The other tables were beginning to fill up and Minna was busy now. Nicole could tell that she was watching Connor all the time, though he didn't appear to notice.

'So,' he said when Minna had brought his coffee and another for Nicole. 'Are we in business?'

'We are. It's a great idea, Connor.'

'That's what the powers-that-be at the Melrose Gallery thought too.' He sounded fully satisfied and she smiled at his enthusiasm.

'When would you plan to start?'

'Tomorrow week?'

'Why not?'

'Not too soon?'

It could never be too soon, she thought. The anticipation would make the week ahead drag for her. But she must act in a businesslike manner, and not let on how breathless she felt every time Connor looked at her in that heart-stopping way. 'I'll be ready,' she promised.

Louise and Jem would have gone home by then, giving her ample time to prepare the room for more guests. She would start working out dinner menus straight away. There was a lot to think about.

Connor raised his cup to his lips and then put it down again. 'Two weeks initially,' he said. 'We'll see how it works out. I hope that's satisfactory?'

She nodded. It had to be. This wasn't the moment to quibble.

'Each course will last five days, Monday to Friday, accommodation required Monday to Saturday morning, and we'll have the weekends to ourselves. Between us we'll get it sorted, won't we?'

She gave out a breath of pure pleasure. 'Oh, yes.'

He smiled brilliantly, a shaft of fitful sunshine highlighting his hair for just a second. It seemed a good omen, and yes, she was satisfied with that. They talked of how each day would be different for the painters with varying locations, weather permitting. It all sounded so interesting that Nicole, like Minna, wished that she could take part herself.

And so it was settled. As soon as the first firm booking for accommodation came in, Connor would notify her.

He drained the rest of his coffee and got up. 'Now I must get back to work before my gear is carried away by the tide.'

She wanted him to suggest that she went with him, but she could see that it wouldn't do. His mind was far away now, intent on his work. She watched him stride off towards the rocks and, when he was out of sight, got up too.

It wasn't until she was on her way back along the path to Cornerstone that Nicole contemplated what she had taken on with some misgivings. The first flush of enthusiasm had waned a little now as she began to think of the practicalities. She would need to sort out more chairs for the stone hut, and maybe tables too, although Connor had assured her the painters would provide their own easels. Lighting might be a problem on dull days because electricity wasn't laid on. Perhaps it would be possible to run a cable across the lane and provide table lamps? She must think about that. There were lists to draw up of what must be done. She wasn't afraid of hard work, but only of the task of pleasing so many different people with the meals she produced. And, above all, of pleasing Connor.

How lucky his students were to have the chance to work with a master like Connor Delaney. That was what they were coming for, not for gourmet meals, although she would like to think hers might reach a high standard. She mustn't let personal pride get in the way, though. She would just do her best. Maybe she could get Sophie's help with the evening meals? Now, that was an idea.

Happier now, she resolved to call at the Penberthy home after lunch and put her proposition to the girl's parents.

★ ★ ★

The Penberthy family lived in the end house of the row of terraced cottages in Treloose, but at the opposite end to Daniel's home. Eddy Penberthy came to the door, rubbing his hands on a brightly-coloured towel and calling out to his wife as to the whereabouts of their daughter.

'She's out, I'm afraid,' he said to Nicole. 'You could leave a message.'

Nicole explained her errand, emphasising that it was only an idea she wanted to run past Sophie's parents first.

'Then you'd better come in,' he said.

Sophie's mother was very like her daughter, with the same quick movements and a way of looking at people expectantly, with her hands clutched together, as if some momentous piece of news was about to be divulged.

'I'm sorry to interrupt anything,' Nicole said, smiling at her.

The room they were in was the kitchen, a long, narrow room at the front of the house, smelling of the aftermath of Sunday lunch. Two damp tea towels hung limply from a clothes airer hanging from the ceiling.

It was Joe Penberthy who motioned

Nicole to one of the chairs at the table. As she sat down the others did too, and Joe pushed an open newspaper to one side.

'She's got school,' her mother said doubtfully when Nicole had told her why she was here.

'That's why I wanted to talk to you first.'

'Good of you,' said Joe. 'Don't you think so, Anna?'

Anna Penberthy smiled and her face lit up with a suddenness that was charming.

'End of term soon,' said Eddy. 'I don't see it would hurt her to do a bit of washing-up.'

'And waiting at tables,' said Nicole. 'I wouldn't keep her late.'

They seemed perfectly amenable to her suggestion, with the proviso that Sophie must decide for herself. Nicole left them with a feeling of pleasure.

Sophie called round later in the afternoon, full of gratitude and enthusiasm for the evening job being offered to her. She had been out earlier, and although her parents had shown their approval, she'd wanted to come round at once to find out what was involved.

'No problem,' Sophie said, once Nicole had explained. 'I'm only working at the Shack on Saturdays.'

'What about your schoolwork?'

'The exams are nearly over. We don't do a lot for the last weeks. I'll be all right.'

'You're sure? Of course, we don't know yet exactly how it will work out, but it could be a good thing for all of us.'

They were sitting out at the back of the stone hut on an old bench that Nicole had brought over from her overgrown garden across the lane. It was pleasant here in the sunshine and neither was anxious to move.

'I'll run you home, Sophie,' Nicole said at last.

She got up and stretched. Life was looking good with the summer stretching before her in such an interesting way — so why did she have this tiny of niggle of concern deep down? Everything was snapping into place in a way she could hardly have imagined. Best of all, she had been able to do something for Connor that he appreciated, and which in some small way must have made up to him for her grandparents' treatment of him in the past.

And yet . . .

She sighed. Tiredness, that was all. She'd take it easy for the rest of the day; prepare a light meal on a tray to carry it into the front room to eat in front of the TV. And then to bed early so she would feel invigorated tomorrow, ready to cook a magnificent breakfast for Louise and Jem as they began their last week's holiday here in Polvanion.

# 12

As Nicole came out of the Post Office the next day, blinking in the bright sunlight, she was surprised to see Daniel talking to someone she recognised as the elderly lady she had seen at the Penvenna Hotel when she and Connor were dining there. She had noticed her then for the elegant way she moved from door to table, and her smile of appreciation as the waiter pulled out her chair for her.

Daniel looked up and saw Nicole. He was wearing a light suit with an open-necked cream shirt, and looked taller and older somehow than he did in his casual clothes. She felt strangely shy of him as he greeted her.

'Nicole,' he said with pleasure.

Mrs Landon smiled too as they were introduced. 'Daniel has been showing me where he keeps his boat,' she said.

'Such a charming little anchorage for it.'

'So it is on a glorious day like this,' he said. 'I've been trying to persuade Mrs Landon to take a trip out with me, Nicole, but she won't have anything to do with it.'

Mrs Landon shuddered. 'Certainly not with you dressed in those clothes.'

He grinned at her and then looked down at them as if surprised not to find himself in his usual shorts and T-shirt. 'You think I'm not capable of steering a boat dressed like this? Well, you may be right. Suitable for a meeting in Truro, though, you must admit that.'

'I admit nothing,' said Mrs Landon.

'That's unlike you!'

'Is it now, dear boy? How's this, then? The sooner you get out of those clothes and into your rough old working things, the better. You've work to do, and not only for me if I know anything about it.'

'If you say so, ma'am.'

Nicole laughed, liking the light-hearted banter between the two of them. They obviously got on well and were on the same wavelength as to furniture renewal. She remembered now where she had first heard him mention Mrs Landon — it was when he had shown her his workshop. She wondered how that lovely piece of furniture was looking in its new home.

'I take it you won't object to the last few miles in my car, however I'm dressed?' Daniel said.

'And there you're wrong. I shall walk back across the beach and save you the drive round by road. That is, of course, if I can find the way to it from here.'

'I'll show you,' Nicole said. 'I'm on my way along the coast in that direction anyway.'

'That's kind of you, dear. And thank you for the lift from Truro, Daniel. I'm truly grateful.'

As they walked through the village to join the coastal path, Mrs Landon chatted about how she had come to meet Daniel a year or two ago when she answered his advertisement about furniture renewal.

'I was intrigued by the word 'renewal' instead of the more usual 'restoration',' she said. 'I had some old and rather decrepit pieces, so I decided to see what he could do. Nothing to lose, I thought. How right I was. He's an artist, that young man, no doubt about it. He deserves to do well.'

'I saw a chest of drawers, a small one, he'd been working on for you,' Nicole said as they walked past the last of the shops. 'Dove-grey and turquoise, with a little silver on the edges. I thought it was charming.'

'It looks well in my long, low sitting room,' Mrs Landon said. 'But soon it will have a new home I hope it will like as much. I decided to downsize, you see, and my house in Truro is being sold.'

'But you're not moving right away from the area?'

They had reached the path now that would take them along past the Shack and down to the beach. Because they were walking in single file, Mrs Landon didn't reply for a moment. Then she paused and looked back the way they had come, as if checking the route for future use. As she glanced at Nicole, her grey eyes looked mischievous.

'I hope you don't think I'm a mad old woman, dear, but I'm on my way to stay in my new property now as a paying guest for a week or two until my own wing there is ready for occupation.'

'You are?' Nicole was surprised. There were no other buildings on the land that came to an end on the other side of the beach. No other building, that was, except the Penvenna Hotel, set back from the narrow lane in its own extensive grounds.

'You see, dear, I bought the hotel.'

'The *hotel*?'

Mrs Landon laughed, a happy sound in the still air. 'Yes, the hotel. I've shocked you, I can see.'

'But you say you've downsized?'

'Well, yes, in a way. But I don't wonder you're surprised.'

Nicole was certainly that. It silenced

181

her for all of five minutes.

They continued to walk, passing the Shack. As they reached the bottom of the path Mrs Landon turned to look at the ramshackle building, frowning. 'I wonder they don't demolish that and build something more substantial. It must be a goldmine all through the season.'

'It belongs to the council,' Nicole said. 'There's a rumour going about that they want to take it down as it's in such a poor condition. I heard it in the Post Office just now. They think the beach should be returned to how it was years ago.'

'To live in the past, you mean? Taking a backward step is never good in my opinion.'

'They don't want anything modern here, apparently.'

'They call that decrepit place modern?'

Mrs Landon had such an expression of disapproval on her face that Nicole laughed, and then they were both laughing. It was well there was no one else there to see them, Nicole thought as she wiped the tears from her eyes.

'I'd ask you to come all the way with me and join me in afternoon tea,' Mrs Landon said at last. 'But I'm in the process of moving some of my belongings in, personal things you know, and I need to see to that. I hope you'll come another time?'

'I'd like that.'

'Then you must give me your telephone number so we can make an arrangement.'

Nicole was still finding Mrs Landon's purchase of the hotel hard to take in. Seeing this, Mrs Landon smiled. 'I'm glad to say that the manager is happy to stay on to run the place for me,' she said. 'And all the staff are staying too. I shall just sit back and enjoy myself. It seemed a good investment, and a perfect thing to do as I want to be by the sea. I'd like to show you round the small wing I'm going to be occupying when the sale is completed.'

'I think I saw you in the hotel dining room the other evening.'

'You did?'

'I was there with an old friend. We'd lost touch over the years.'

'So it was good to meet again?'

'Oh yes.' To her horror Nicole felt herself blush.

Mrs Landon smiled. 'Now you come to mention it, I think I saw you too. You were with the artist who's staying there. Colin Delaney, isn't it?'

'Connor,' said Nicole.

'Ah yes, Connor Delaney whose exhibition in Truro had to be cancelled.'

Nicole hesitated. She hadn't asked him the reason, but knew there was talk of it being restaged in the autumn. When she mentioned it Mrs Landon looked a little sceptical. 'Is that so?' she said.

Nicole started to tell her about the classes Connor would be organising in the stone hut and how this would benefit her B&B business.

'I had some property of his,' she said quickly. 'Paintings. We're going to be working together. I mean . . .' Aware that she was gabbling, she paused to take a breath

Mrs Landon smiled. 'I've been hearing that he had to leave Polvanion years ago after he'd been living and working there. Something about the building he was renting not having planning permission to be used as a residence, and the legalities only being discovered after he had settled in. So the unfortunate man had to be given notice.'

'Oh no, I don't think it was quite like that.' Nicole said. 'It belonged to my grandparents, you see. I never heard that that was the reason he went so quickly.'

'Ah well, I don't suppose it matters much now.'

Nicole was silent. She supposed it didn't matter in the great scheme of things, but it had mattered to her desperately at the time. Even now, she didn't like to think that her normally kind grandfather had been callous when he insisted Connor leave at once.

'Well now, I mustn't keep you, dear,' Mrs Landon said. 'Thank you so much for showing me the way. Oh, I nearly forgot!'

'My phone number?' said Nicole, feeling in her pocket for a pen and paper. 'It wouldn't do to forget to give you that.'

'Indeed not. Thank you, my dear. Enjoy your walk.'

* * *

Nicole stopped at the Shack on her way home, feeling the need for one of Minna's mugs of strong coffee. She ordered a pasty too.

'Something wrong?' Minna asked when she had brought it. She perched on the side of the long wooden table and swung her leg backwards and forwards.

'Should there be?'

'You tell me.'

Nicole wished she could, but this was a private matter. Mrs Landon must have got it wrong when she said that the reason for Grandpop evicting Connor from the stone hut was because it wasn't possible for him to live there legally. It wasn't like that. It meant that someone had been talking who hadn't had the true facts. She hadn't asked Connor about it when she saw him along the coastal path just now. For one thing, she was surprised to see him with his sketching gear.

He had looked pleased to see her, and paused in what he was doing as she came round the corner and saw ahead of her the rocky coastline with its indents in the low cliffs. It was here on a grassy mound that Connor was seated with his gear spread out round him.

She saw that a page of his sketch-book, open on his lap, was covered in charcoal lines and smudges. He tapped the ground beside him. 'Sit down, my love. You look tired. I've been doing some recce. A perfect spot for a day's sketching. I've found one or two back there as well. Useful for painting outdoors with the students.'

'*En plein air*,' she said as she sat down beside him.

He laughed his deep, throaty laugh, and the expression in his eyes was unreadable. She took a deep breath and moved away slightly. By the way the sun had caught his face it seemed he must have been here for some time, although she remembered that his skin burnt easily.

He turned a page in his sketchbook, and with a few deft strokes drew the shape of the rocks down below them where the water lapped and then withdrew in little gentle swathes time and again. The larks were busy in the air above them in twittering song, just as it had been on Chapel Head, but this time she was with Connor and the afternoon air was warm with the scent of bruised grass.

This was no moment to raise painful memories of the past and the inaccuracies of the present. The mood of this quiet place on the edge of the sea was peaceful and full of promise.

He gave her a sideways look, his charcoal still busy. 'Happy?'

'Oh, yes.'

Who wouldn't be happy in this lovely place, with the man she was pleased to get to know again after all these years? It was an idyllic moment and one she wanted to impress on her memory.

But it ended soon after. They heard the voices before they saw the group of walkers coming cheerfully round an outcrop of rocks, calling out to each other and pointing with their sticks at something they saw in the water down below. They looked hot and happy as they went on their way, the ground seeming to rock beneath their feet with the exuberance of it all. Even when they had passed the air seemed full of their presence.

Connor got up and began to pack his gear away in his canvas bag, his attention on the job in hand. Nicole watched for a moment and then got up too.

Even now, sitting at one of the Shack's long tables, Nicole felt bruised, as if they had done her a physical injury.

★  ★  ★

Nicole knew the workload would be hard, but she hadn't bargained for the vagaries of the students who had booked her rooms. It must be the artistic temperament, she told herself on the third day when three of them didn't turn up for the evening meal. Then another declined breakfast the following morning, opting to remain in bed until ten o'clock and then rush out just in time for that day's programme to begin, without checking the equipment he needed for a day away from the studio. The twin bedroom, when she could finally get in to make his bed, was a shambles.

The packed lunches were all done before breakfast because Connor had planned a day's sketching at Chapel

Head and wanted to get off at immediately. For some reason he seemed to blame Nicole for both the delay and the unkempt appearance of the sixty-year-old man who was proving so difficult.

She was left feeling exhausted, even though she had done very few of the tasks planned for the day. Supermarket shopping, for one. She had thought she had got well-stocked before they came, but now she discovered she needed other fruit juices for breakfast beside orange and pineapple, and that her estimate of bread and rolls needed was way off-target.

First, though, she must go the Post Office and buy stamps, in case there should be some autumn bookings that needed receipts for deposits when the place was closed. Not that there had been, yet, and that was slightly worrying. Connor hadn't told her how things were going.

Mrs Pascoe looked at Nicole in concern when she went in, jangling shut the door behind her.

'Is everything all right, m'dear?'

Nicole did her best to smile. 'Oh yes.'

'Joe Penberthy was saying young Sophie's in her element along there at Cornerstone. Working her hard, are you?'

'As hard as I dare.'

'You're a kind employer, I'm sure, m'dear.'

Nicole laughed. 'Little do you know.' In fact, she was considering keeping Sophie confined to the kitchen in future, not liking the way Connor made a fuss of her that was making Sophie a bit above herself. But who was she to spoil things for the girl?

★ ★ ★

By ten o'clock on Saturday morning the first week's students had all departed, two of them after dinner the evening before. The second load of sheets and duvet covers was in the washing machine, and Nicole had remade all the beds and made a start on cleaning the double bedroom. She had been disappointed that Connor hadn't suggested meeting this weekend, but understood that he was off to visit a colleague on the Lizard who had recently been bereaved.

Connor had shrugged apologetically when he told her, as she saw him briefly after the finish of the day's session yesterday. 'But at least there's some good news,' he had said. 'Bookings have come in for a third week's course, and it's nearly full for the one following, too. I shan't go out of business yet awhile.'

Of course that was good news, but Nicole felt slightly cheated not to be seeing anything of him during the weekend. So when Mrs Landon telephoned to say that she had tickets for the preview of Kirk Andrew's exhibition at the Melrose Gallery on Saturday evening, and would Nicole like to accompany her, she was delighted to accept.

'I shall order a taxi and pick you up at six-thirty,' Mrs Landon said. 'That will give us plenty of time.'

'Not a bit of it,' Nicole said. 'Far nicer for me to drive.'

'But that means you can't drink, my dear.'

'No problem. Orange juice for me — or perhaps something more exotic and non-alcoholic if they can come up with it.'

'Mrs Landon laughed. 'We'll see what they can do.'

In the event, they didn't stay much longer than it took to examine all the paintings on display — when they could get near enough to catch a glimpse of them through the crowds of people who also had invitations.

Nicole found a seat for her companion in the room set aside for the excellent buffet and brought a plate of canapés to her.

'They must have been expecting thousands to turn up,' Mrs Landon said in disgust as this room became overcrowded too. She finished eating, placed her empty plate on a side table and stood up. 'I'm sorry it was such a crush, my dear, but these things often are. Shall we go?'

Nicole was only too pleased to leave now. She would return when the exhibition opened for a closer look at the work that, at brief glance, had seemed interesting. Connor's cancelled preview might have been the same crush, she thought, as they walked slowly back to the car. She might not have had the chance after all to speak to him about the forgotten paintings.

Mrs Landon seemed happy enough with her evening out and invited Nicole to have coffee with her on the terrace when they got back to the hotel. Afterwards she showed her round the part of the building that was to be her future home, pleased at Nicole's admiring reaction to it.

'And I'm keeping that old building near the gate for my own use,' Mrs Landon said. 'It seemed wise. I might need it for storage, you know? Down-sizing can be a bit of a problem in many ways. Or I might find some other use for it.'

On the way in Nicole had noticed the long, low building with a tiled mossy roof that seemed settled into the surrounding ground as if it had been there for generations — perhaps it had. There was a larger-than-usual door and three wide windows in the front.

'I'm getting the place cleared out,' Mrs Landon said. 'There is a lot of unused furniture in there, and old unwanted things.'

A little like the stone hut, Nicole thought.

# 13

The second week of Connor's course was much easier for Nicole. For one thing, her guests were all much more pleasant and appreciative of their accommodation. On Tuesday evening, Sophie was late arriving, but one of the younger men, Rory Adams, sprang up from his seat at the dining table to help Nicole with the serving. His eagerness was appealing, and by the time a flustered Sophie appeared, the first course was finished and cleared and Rory was standing by with a clean tea towel over one shoulder, ready to carry in the next.

'So you're our errant waitress?' he said, smiling, when Sophie, flushed and apologetic, burst into the kitchen. 'I think you've lost your job.'

When he had picked up the warmed plates to carry in, Sophie turned an anxious face to Nicole, who was busy straining vegetables. 'He didn't mean it?'

Nicole laughed. 'What d'you think?'

'I'll stay later than usual. I'll lay the breakfast when they've finished. I'll do anything . . . '

'Relax, Sophie. Rory's being helpful, that's all. He's enjoying himself.'

Sophie clutched her hands together so tightly the knuckles showed white. 'You see, Dad had an accident. He fell off the stepladder in the kitchen. I went with them to Accident and Emergency and we got caught in a traffic hold-up at Trensilva on the way back, and . . . '

'He's all right now?'

Just as Sophie was explaining that his ankle was badly sprained but not broken, there was a burst of laughter from the dining room as the door opened. Before Rory had a chance to get back to the kitchen, Sophie grabbed the vegetable dish and bore it off.

Nicole smiled. This was the time of day she enjoyed most. Her guests had

had a good time with Connor, sketching by the harbour in the sunshine. They ate their packed lunches down there too, until it was time to return to the stone hut for more tuition before making a start on their paintings. There were one or two talented artists among them, and Connor called Nicole across to see the standard of the work being produced.

In his bright blue painting smock he looked every inch the part of the confident tutor, moving with encouraging words from one person to another. Nicole could see how much they were all enjoying themselves, and smiled to see the older man among them so engrossed in his harbour scene that Connor stood unnoticed beside him. She went closer to look as Connor moved away towards one of the younger girls tasking part this week.

'Acrylic,' the man, Colin, murmured out of the corner of his mouth. 'No messy oils for me.'

His tubes of paint were arranged in

colour order on the small table at his side, and his small collection of brushes were standing to attention in a clean jar.

'Neat and tidy; that's you, isn't it, Dad?' Rory said with a laugh.

Nicole looked closer at the canvas. No splashing-on of colour here, but carefully-applied paint. Every detail of the boats in the harbour was done with precision. So different from Connor's work, and that of some of the other students who were obviously trying to emulate him.

'It's charming,' she said.

'Thank you, my dear.'

Rory winked at her. Nicole ignored him and looked again at his father's painting. This time she noticed that in the bows of one of the boats at anchor was someone coiling rope. It was Daniel to the life, and she smiled to see it.

Connor was back now looking appraisingly at the painting. 'Don't I recognise someone there, the chap that's always hanging round the place?'

'Daniel Logan,' Nicole had said, still smiling. 'A good likeness, don't you think?'

Connor frowned. 'If you say so.'

Nicole hadn't stayed long after that as there were preparations to be made for the evening meal. But all the time she was slicing mushrooms and onions she thought of Connor's expression and wondered. Now, though, she felt as happy and relaxed as her guests. Tomorrow promised to be a good day too, with an invitation for her to join them on their outing.

★   ★   ★

The minibus joined the main road to St Austell and Nicole leaned back in her seat beside Connor at the front, on the opposite side to the driver, unable to believe this was really happening. Outside, the sky looked fairly ominous, but that didn't dampen the spirits of the six students. All their painting and sketching gear was stored on the seats at the back of the vehicle, and so were the packed lunches Nicole had prepared for the whole group today.

'The Craftie Fayre on Bodmin Moor?' she had said in surprise when her four guests seated themselves in the dining room yesterday evening.

Rory grinned at her. 'A good idea or what?'

'It's a long way.'

'Not far in the bus. We're to spend the day making sketches of everything we see; and painting them, too, if we have the time. It'll be great. And you're to come with us. Connor insists on that, and you can't go against the great master.' There was a faintly ironic tone to his voice and Nicole suppressed a smile.

Once she had got over her surprise she thought the plan a good one. Connor's group would see some of the countryside, and would no doubt find plenty of scope for quick sketches of people enjoying themselves away from their everyday lives. She hadn't been to the Craftie Fayre since she was a child. It was a huge annual event, and people came from far and wide to be there on the first Thursday in July.

Connor turned to her and smiled. 'Happy?'

'Oh, yes.'

'We'll leave them to it after they've got settled. A bit of a chat to start with, a few useful pointers, and then they're away.'

'Sounds good, as long as you don't expect me to embark on a masterpiece too.'

His eyes twinkled at her. 'I think that might be going a bit too far.'

'But what about you? Don't you want to paint?'

'And leave you on your own?'

'There will be plenty to do.'

He said nothing to that but took hold of her hand and pressed it.

★ ★ ★

'You need a good half-hour to wander about getting the feel of things,' Connor had told the group clustering round the parked minibus when he talked to them briefly of his expectations for today. 'People in action' was the theme, portraying movement in such a way that the observer would feel they were drawn into the picture and were part of the scene too. 'Concentrate on the atmosphere, the excitement, the antici- pation . . . '

'The smell?' Rory said.

Connor looked at him with approval. 'That too. The five senses.'

'Time for a coffee first?' asked an elderly lady in a pink kaftan.

Connor looked at her, frowning. 'A quick one only then, Margery, on the move if possible. We won't have longer than six hours here so make the most of them. Take your packed lunches with you, please.'

'Yes, siree,' Rory said, obviously keen to be off but hovering near his father.

Colin put his packet of food into his

painting bag and then hoisted it up on his shoulder. 'Don't mind me, son. You carry on.'

Nicole walked with Connor through the rows of parked vehicles towards the colourful and noisy scene ahead. She wondered how she would have coped with the sketching exercise. It seemed a tall order, as people weren't keeping still for long. But all the students were so talented, even Margery, with her air of fragility that Nicole suspected was exaggerated.

'Coffee for us, Nicole?' Connor said with a lift of his eyebrows.

She smiled. 'Yes please.'

They found a secluded mobile unit specialising in herbal teas and luscious-looking quiches, whose owner, in bottle-green overall and jaunty wide-brimmed hat, was happy to provide a cafetière of coffee for them. They carried it on a tray with mugs and milk jug to one of the tables set out on a grassy strip beyond. The view over open moorland seemed to go on forever.

Nicole gazed at it, entranced. 'I almost feel I could paint that,' she said.

Connor shuddered as he poured coffee. 'Not as easy as you might think. But no characters in it, thank goodness, asking silly questions. Exhausting.' He handed her one of the mugs and then slid the milk jug towards her. 'We should be secluded enough here from my merry throng.'

'They're a friendly lot.'

'They are, they are. Fingers crossed that each week's selection might be as affable.'

'Drinking in your every word?'

He laughed, more relaxed now. 'Something like that. I have hopes of Colin Adams booking in for another week after this.'

'Rory's father?'

Connor nodded. 'Not Rory, though. He's due back at work, more's the pity.

Nicole thought so too. It would mean a single occupancy instead of double.

'And the local couple are thinking of coming again. They're getting some friends of theirs interested.'

'Local too?'

'Nothing wrong with that.'

No accommodation needed for them then. Nicole took a sip of coffee and then put the mug down again.

'Why so sad?'

She hesitated, not wanting to break this ambience between them with down-to-earth concerns about her need to be financially secure. The rent of the stone hut was useful, but it wasn't enough this far into the season to justify the lack of paying guests. But if she mentioned this to Connor now, his mood would darken and she might just as well have stayed at home.

Connor's satisfaction at their being on their own didn't last long. Margery came past not long afterwards.

'I've sketched a good selection of people already,' she told Connor. 'Now I'm going to find an interesting background for them. I shall plonk them down in it, as it were. I'm allowed to do that, aren't I?'

Connor gave all the appearance of delight as her pronouncement. 'Good girl, Margery. I can see you will be wanting another week with me.'

'I certainly would,' she said. 'You can take that as a firm commitment.'

'There you are, Nicole,' Connor said when Margery had gone tripping off. 'That means another booking for your accommodation too.'

Nicole tried to look pleased. This would be for another single occupancy. Not good from her point of view, but she would have to make the best of it.

The two young girls in the group came to find Connor after that, anxious for him to inspect their work. It was time for Nicole to leave them to it and take a look around on her own.

She wandered among the stalls and amused herself by concentrating on the five senses. Sight was easy because of the myriad colours of the bright canopies and the goods displayed on the stalls. Smell was, too, from the crushed grass and burgers being sizzled on a grill nearby. There was plenty of sound from the barrel organ and the traction engine, children's squeals and laughter, and the booming voice of an auctioneer with his selection before him of unlikely objects. He held a decorated wellington boot high in the air, inviting bids of a sensible nature that had the crowd jeering at him with bursts of laughter. Touch? The rough feel of the empty pink sea urchin shells on the stall laden with shells from around the world was pleasing. And the fifth sense? She would have to think about that.

She caught sight of Connor eating a sandwich as he moved from student to student, totally engrossed now. Nicole found a quiet spot out of the wind to eat her own lunch, and afterwards wandered about again. She paused at stalls that caught her fancy and eventually stopped in surprise at seeing Daniel. He was leaning over his table of driftwood creations, talking to a customer so earnestly that he didn't see her. She had time to marvel at the wonderful exhibits before the man moved off, carrying his purchase proudly in front of him.

The intermittent sunshine had given up now and the sky was a uniform grey. They were high up here on the moor and the breeze they had felt earlier had strengthened. Some of the canopies above the stalls were beginning to flap and one of them looked as if it would take off at any moment.

She buttoned her jacket to the neck and moved nearer. 'Daniel?'

Hearing her voice, he looked up.

'Sorry to startle you,' she said. 'How are you doing?'

'Pretty well. I'm thinking of packing up soon. It's good to see you, Nicole. What brings you here, or is that a silly question?'

'Connor's here for the day with his students to do some work on location, and I came with them.'

'But you're not an artist?'

She laughed. 'Not me.'

'Not in the drawing sort of way, I mean.'

'Nor in your way with these imaginative things either. They're very clever.' The one she liked best was of a seagull perched on a rock that he had fashioned from a single piece of wood; it was so cleverly done she could almost feel the bird's thoughts as it prepared to take off again. She picked it up.

'You like that one?'

'I'd like to buy it.'

'It's not for sale.'

'What?'

'It's a present. I'd like you to have it, Nicole. I suspect it would look well in the window of your stone hut.'

She could imagine it there too but she hesitated. 'I can't . . . '

'You can.' He fished a piece of tissue paper out from under the table and began wrapping it. 'I'm not selling it to anyone else and I haven't room for it back home. The nearest bin it will have to be, then!'

'You don't mean it?'

'I mean everything I say.'

He looked so sure of himself,

standing there looking at her with his head held a little to one side, that she could believe it. 'I think you've convinced me,' she said.

'There's a catch, though.'

She could feel drizzle in the air now. 'You want me to help you pack up?'

'Got it in one. Rain doesn't do these things much good, or me either.'

He had a stash of boxes beneath the table and he got them out swiftly. Each of the items, of all shapes and sizes, needed wrapping to protect them.

They set to work at once. The rain now was coming down faster, bouncing off the emptying table top. Nicole heard a low rumble of thunder in the distance. By the time they had finished they had water streaming down their faces, but the rain was easing a little now.

'Now to get them to the car,' Daniel said.

Nicole wiped her arm across her forehead. 'How far away is it?'

'Quite near. No need for you to worry about that. I can manage.'

She ignored him. Going even a short distance with this load would be tricky with the muddy ground underfoot. She picked up the nearest box. 'Lead on.'

Daniel grinned at her. 'You're as stubborn as me.'

Some of the canopied stalls were still trading, but most were giving up, even though there were crowds of people still about, peeling off their wet outer garments and shaking umbrellas. Daniel's car was parked in a convenient spot near the entrance to the site, away from most of the mud. She looked across at the minibus and saw that it was hemmed in by rows of vehicles.

She shivered as she handed Daniel her last box.

'Cold?' he said. 'You could come back with me.'

His offer was tempting. She had planned quiche and salad for the meal this evening. Now she thought she would make a soup as a starter. The extra time would be useful. She looked across to the minibus. A few students were already there, and Connor was helping them in with their gear.

'I'd better not,' she said.

Daniel nodded. 'Watch your step, then. The ground's a quagmire.'

One or two of the vehicles, splattering mud, were making a hard job of it. She looked back and saw that Daniel was still watching her.

Connor glanced at his watch. 'You haven't seen Lottie and Josie?'

'They're not here?'

'I wouldn't be asking if they were.' His tone was sharp.

She flushed. Stupid question.

'They'll make us late,' he said. 'My dinner's at seven.'

'But you don't have to cook it.'

He hesitated and then smiled. 'Point taken. My poor Nicole.'

She didn't like his tone; it sounded as if he were making fun of her. 'I've had the offer of a lift home,' she said. 'I could use the extra time.'

'Off you go, then.'

'You don't mind?'

'Just remember you're my little playmate, not his.'

'You've said that before.'

'That's because I mean it.'

She made her way back to Daniel, who opened the passenger door for her.

'Permission?' he said.

'What did you expect?'

He grinned but said nothing.

'This is kind of you, Daniel.'

It took only seconds to get the van through the entrance, and then they were on the road and away.

# 14

They spoke little as they travelled in a stream of cars on the A30, bypassing Bodmin, but Nicole had the impression that Daniel was relieved to have her with him. His hands were light on the steering wheel and he smiled a great deal. She sat back in her seat and relaxed.

The clouds were clearing a little now, but the trees on the lower ground were still heavy with water. Everything looked fresher and less dreary than on the way up — and yet this really couldn't be, Nicole thought. They'd had a heavy rain shower that was all. The countryside was the same.

She was still pondering this when they reached the outskirts of St Austell and took the road to Polvanion.

'Not long now,' Daniel said.

She thought of his small cottage near the cliff top at Treloose and the lonely makeshift meal which she imagined awaited him.

'You'll stay for a meal with us?' she said. 'Please do, Daniel. I'll be sitting down with the guests tonight, and we'd be glad to have you with us.'

'Well . . .'

'Connor won't be there. He's having dinner at his hotel.'

'In that case, then, thanks. I'll nip home after I've dropped you off, and change out of these wet things, but I won't be long.'

'We'll warm ourselves up with hot drinks while I get the soup on.'

'Sounds brilliant.'

She was glad she had suggested it.

A quick shower and hairwash. Then a hasty look through her wardrobe to find her black slimline trousers and cream shirt, and she was ready to get started on the meal. With a towel, she rubbed her hair hard and then left it to dry at its own speed. Daniel wouldn't mind . . . and yet she would have got the hairdryer out at once if she was expecting Connor.

The quiches were warming in the oven by the time Daniel arrived, the salad made, and new potatoes ready to put on the stove.

Daniel wrinkled his nose as he followed her into the kitchen. 'Something smells good.'

'Carrot and coriander soup. Like some?'

'Homemade? That can't be bad.'

She had put his gift of the wooden seagull on the windowsill in here for the time being, and she saw him looking at it.

'That's its temporary home,' she told him. When the stone hut feels like my own again, that's where it will live.'

'I'd like to see it there.'

'One day.'

His eyes looked bright. 'I'll hold you to that.'

There was the sound of footsteps outside the back door now, and the next moment Sophie appeared. 'I'm not late, am I?'

Daniel glanced at his watch. 'You'd get the push if I were Nicole.'

She made a face at him. 'But you're not.'

'Lucky, then, aren't you?' He smiled cheerfully at his young relative. 'I'm an honoured guest here, I'd have you know.'

Sophie looked at Nicole for confirmation.

Nicole nodded. 'You didn't think he'd gatecrashed? The others will be here soon. Like to lay the table, Sophie?'

'Only if Uncle Dan helps me.'

'Cousin Dan, please.'

'Second Cousin Dan, then, if you want to be picky.'

'I'm always picky,' he said.

'Unlike some.'

'And who might that be?'

But Sophie wouldn't say. She turned her back on him and fished some cutlery out of the drawer.

While they were busy gently sparring, Nicole poured three bowls of soup; and by the time Rory and his father arrived, closely followed by Margery and her husband, Sophie was washing the empty bowls at the sink ready for them to be used again.

Earlier, Connor's students had taken shelter from the rain, and so these four had no need to change. They were all soon seated in the dining room with the table extended for six. Sophie, an adept waitress, did all that was necessary, and had the dishes and cutlery from the first two courses washed up by the time the apple pie needed to be brought in.

'No one would think you'd spent the day with us, Nicole,' Colin Adams said. 'That was an excellent meal. Thank you, my dear.'

Margery's husband smiled. 'We're going to miss this wonderful cuisine when we get home.'

'Not me, Tom,' Margery said. 'I'll be here again, don't forget.'

Daniel looked interested. 'For a second week?'

'Connor suggested it. You want to

stay on too, don't you, Colin?'

They talked a little about this because Daniel wanted to know how they intended employing their time over the weekend before the tuition started again on Monday. In the end, it was decided to take him up on his offer of boat trips down the coast for some sketching practice in different locations.

Nicole was grateful for Daniel's thoughtful input. The extra two-night booking was useful — especially as Margery and Colin would be full board, needing packed lunches as they had all week — but she looked forward to having the house to herself for the two days. It sounded as if both of them would be fully occupied in an enjoyable way, and that was good.

*　★　★*

Nicole stood up straight to ease her back after scrubbing the cord carpet in the stone hut on Saturday morning. Someone had upset some acrylic paint and not cleaned it up with water immediately. Now the dark green stain had hardened and was difficult to move. Colin and Margery's painting gear was still here, of course, Colin's neatly packed in his bag and his easel folded and placed out of the way. Margery's box of paints was balanced on her easel in the centre of the room and had looked about to come crashing down. Nicole had placed it for safety on the table Connor used for his sketch books and teaching notes.

The others had departed soon after breakfast and she expected Connor to arrive at any moment to tell her the plans for the week. She'd wanted the stone hut to be at least presentable when he came, and had worked hard.

Instead, it was Daniel who pushed open the door and came in on a breath of salty air.

'I've got Mrs Landon outside,' he told her. 'OK if I bring her in?'

'Of course it is.' Nicole smiled and moved her bucket out of the way.

Surely she wasn't wanting to sign up for one of Connor's courses?

'I've caught you at a bad moment,' Mrs Landon said.

'Of course you haven't. I've just finished. What d'you think?'

Mrs Landon came inside and looked round in appreciation. 'What a charming room. And such a view. Have you a few moments to spare, my dear?'

At once, Nicole pulled forward two of the chairs. 'Plenty of time.'

Daniel, smiling, gave her a salute. 'I'll see you later. Work calls.' And he was gone.

'Work?' said Mrs Landon.

'He's taking two of my guests out in his boat for the day,' Nicole said.

'Ah, yes. I believe he said.' She seated herself and looked at Nicole kindly. 'Aren't you going to sit down too? I have a message from a friend of yours. It was to tell you that he's been called away and not to expect him after all. He knew I was coming into Polvanion, you see. He tried to phone and got no answer.'

'Oh.' There was a wealth of desolation in that one word, but it was too late to sound positive now.

'You're disappointed?'

'Well, yes, a bit.'

'Then I have a suggestion. If you're free this afternoon, I should so like you to take afternoon tea with me at the hotel.'

She looked so expectant sitting there on the hard upright chair that Nicole was touched. She had seen to the guest's bedrooms earlier, and the preparations for the evening meal were in place.

'I should like that very much,' she said,

'Then I shall expect you about three o'clock, my dear.'

The afternoon was so warm and sunny that, when the time came for Nicole to walk across the beach to the Penvenna Hotel, she found that Mrs Landon had arranged to have tea served on the lawn in the shade of a sycamore tree.

They talked gently of Connor's painting classes and of the students that found them so fascinating.

'Minna, the nice part-time reception-ist here, seemed to know a lot about them,' Mrs Landon said. 'We had quite a chat. Apparently Connor's already beginning to lose his enthusiasm for what he's doing here. It's the same course every week, you see, so it's bound to seem monotonous at times.'

'But mainly with different students.'

'There's that, of course. But he's so talented himself that he's sure to find it hard dealing with amateurs. He's gone with two of them for a day in Plymouth, apparently; though why Minna should find that upsetting wasn't clear.'

Lottie and Josie? It had to be. Nicole's heart felt sore that he hadn't confided in her, since she was involved with his project. But no doubt a man like Connor wouldn't have thought of that.

'More tea, my dear?'

'Thank you.' Nicole's hand trembled a little as she passed her cup and saucer across, but Mrs Landon appeared to notice nothing.

'So Daniel has taken up boat trips now, I understand?' she said. 'A new career, d'you suppose? Minna wasn't clear on that either.'

Nicole giggled. 'He's taken my two elderly guests on a sketching trip today, and he's planning another for tomorrow.'

Mrs Landon nodded. 'That will keep his mind occupied while he's waiting for a decision about a suitable showroom.'

Nicole sat up straight. 'He is?'

Mrs Landon's smile was enigmatic. Since she seemed disinclined to say more, Nicole let the subject drop.

★  ★  ★

Margery and Colin felt like old friends to Nicole now, and the following week should have been easier. By now, Nicole knew she should be used to rising at an early hour and getting breakfast underway. Perhaps it was her fear that things weren't going quite as well as Connor had predicted that made her spirits low.

Connor admitted that bookings were tailing off when he called in to the cottage after giving his students another harbour assignment on Friday morning. He looked different in his subdued jersey and faded jeans. Mrs Landon had said he had lost some of his enthusiasm, and today Nicole could believe it.

'We must cheer ourselves up,' he told her. 'What do you say to us leaving my lot to it after lunch and going off somewhere by ourselves?'

'Their last afternoon?'

'Why not?'

'If you're sure?'

'D'you doubt me?'

A surge of joy ran through Nicole that he was seeking her company. She smiled. 'Where will we go?'

'Along the cliffs somewhere? To the

west past Treloose, I think. I've been told there's good rock formations further on.'

'Good for painting?'

He grinned and for a moment was the confident Connor she had come to know. 'That's what I want to find out. A new venue for next week's lot with luck. Mature students, would you believe? They'll be getting a challenge, like it or not. You like watching me work, don't you, Nicole?'

'I hope the weather forecast is good.'

'It will be.'

And it was. Not a cloud in the sky as they set off side by side along the track that narrowed further on as it got closer to the cliff top. Connor had his painting gear in a rucksack slung on his back, and looked full of purpose.

'So what have you told your students?'

'Two have left already.'

'They have?'

'A long way to go. Manchester, or somewhere. And they needed to be back tonight. We parted friends, Nicole. No need to look so worried.'

'And the rest?'

'Finishing off their projects. Studio work for some, down near the harbour for the rest, leaving me to flutter between them with my words of wisdom.'

He looked so pleased with himself that Nicole laughed. 'So each lot will think you're with the others?'

'That's it.'

You had to hand it to him, Nicole thought. It was so unfair that in anyone else this irresponsible behaviour would be disgraceful, but in the glow of Connor Delaney's ebullient personality it could be forgiven. Charm was a dangerous thing.

They were on the higher part of the cliff now near Treloose. Connor paused for a moment and turned to her. 'This looks familiar.'

'You remembered?'

An expression of doubt crossed his face for a moment. Then he smiled.

'How could I forget?'

She was satisfied. They walked on the with the sun high in the sky to their left, and the warm scented air on their skin. The gulls' mournful calls were in the distance. The same ones as those they had heard years ago? It seemed so. Nicole smiled to herself as she tried to work out how many gull generations there were between then and now.

So far, it had seemed that they had the world to themselves, but as they got further on they saw a group of ramblers coming towards them, strung out along the path as they pointed out fresh discoveries to each other. They called cheerful drawn-out greetings to Connor and Nicole, their voices fading as they moved on.

And now they could hear the sound of the sea surging against the base of the cliffs, and smell it, too. Further on, they came to the place they were heading for, where stacks of cliff seemed to have been broken off from the rest and where the sea roared in bursts of sparkling foam.

'This is it,' said Connor in satisfaction.

Instead of seating himself in preparation to sketch, as Nicole had expected, he stood on the edge of the land with his hand shading his eyes, and stared out to sea. She looked, too; she could see nothing to account for his riveted attention, but knew better than to ask.

Several moments passed and then Connor seemed to relax. 'This has been overdone,' he said. 'I can make nothing of it.'

'But surely your students . . . '

'What students?' he said, his voice so full of irritation that she was startled. 'A couple of ninety-year-olds from nearby, too frail to venture out of the studio, and just another chap wanting your accommodation.

'That's all?'

'Can you wonder that I feel I've had enough? What am I doing in Polvanion wasting my time? And now the old woman has changed her mind.'

He muttered something more Nicole couldn't catch. And then there were more people coming towards them, a couple and an elderly man walking with two sticks. They gave every intention of not moving on.

'A beautiful place, isn't it?' the woman said in pleasant tones.

Nicole smiled and agreed, but Connor scowled. 'We'll get out of your way,' he said.

'Oh no, we . . . '

'Come, Nicole,' he said sharply. 'We're not wanted here.'

Her ears tingling with embarrassment, she followed him round the next bend, almost running to keep up with his smart pace.

'Please, Connor . . . '

He swung round. 'Had enough?'

'Of your bad mood?'

He relaxed suddenly. 'You're right as always, dear little Nicole. Like your grandfather, a great sense of right and wrong. A good man, but too honest by half. I have happy memories of his kindness to me in welcoming me to the stone hut.'

'I loved him,' she said simply.

'And I respected him.'

'But he turned you out of the stone hut.' The pain was still there, her beloved grandfather not giving Connor a chance to say goodbye in his haste to get rid of him! And all because of her. It was hard to think of, even now.

'His uprightness was catching, his honesty.'

'Honesty?'

'When he found out he wasn't allowed to use the hut for sleeping in, for his family or anyone else. It was illegal, you see, against the law; although until that moment he was wasn't aware of it.'

She was dumbfounded. She tried to remember how it had been.

'Which moment?' she asked through dry lips. She thought of Connor's last day, of her coming off the school bus in the square and knowing something was wrong as she approached the stone hut. It was too silent, too empty-looking.

She had burst into the cottage and found her grandmother sitting at the table in the kitchen shelling peas.

'Where's Connor?'

'He was angry,' Gran said in her soft voice. 'So angry. He thought he was here for the summer, able to work at his own pace. He wouldn't wait for your Grandpop to see our solicitor to try to arrange an extension for a week or two, or even to pay us the rent he owed.'

'He went off at once?'

'A strange man, my love. An artist, you see. We must make allowances.'

Nicole stood on the cliff path, feeling as cold as stone as she struggled to take this in. No one had told her the true state of affairs, that Connor had left of his own accord with not a word to her. He had gone and she was left desolate.

She didn't go into the stone hut after that. His Paradise Room, Connor had called it, the place where he was working hard to gain the recognition he deserved. And soon after that Gran's health had deteriorated, and it had seemed best for Nicole to live for a while in Bristol with Christa and pursue her education there.

Nothing had mattered anymore as she withdrew into a world of shocked silence. She would do whatever they wanted; her hurt at her grandparents' betrayal, as she had thought it, too deep for words.

Now, like a zombie, she allowed Connor to catch hold of her by the arm and encourage her to move.

'Are you ill?' he said.

'No, no, I . . . '

'Come on, then, let's get out of here.'

He found a footpath leading across fields to a road soon after that; and, pleased that they wouldn't have to return along the increasingly busy coastal path, talked cheerfully about plans he had to move back to Truro in preparation for his autumn exhibition.

They were back in Polvanion before she knew it.

# 15

Margery and Colin's last evening meal was a low-key occasion. They had enjoyed themselves even more this second week, and were sad it had come to an end.

'We shall come back, Jim and me, one day,' Margery promised. 'This time next year, perhaps? That's a date.'

Nicole gave a brief smile and the skin on her face felt strained with the effort. She didn't know now what she would be doing in a year's time. Her return here seemed a ridiculous thing to have done. All the time she was assembling the strawberry pavlova out in the kitchen, she was agonising over having believed that her grandfather had turfed Connor out of the stone hut so peremptorily when he had nowhere else to go. She had thought badly of him all these years when it wasn't true. It was clear from what Mrs Landon said that others hadn't believed it. And yet she, who loved him, had done so.

'You look dreadful,' Sophie said when she returned to the kitchen. 'I mean, you look nice and all that in that blue shirt. But Nicole, d'you think you should go and lie down? I can clear up down here.'

The girl's concern was touching. So that Sophie wouldn't see the tears that sprang to her eyes, Nicole turned her back and ran some hot water into the sink. 'It's all right, Sophie. I'm fine, really. Just a bit tired.'

'That's what Daniel says,' Sophie confided. 'He thinks it's all a bit much for you.'

Nicole swung round. 'So who asked him?'

Sophie shrugged. 'I told him to mind his own business, that I was here to help, and what was wrong with that? But he takes no notice of me.'

Nicole banged down the spoon she was holding. Daniel should keep his opinions to himself; she'd have something to say if he dared suggest anything like that to her.

Her two guests retired early that night, wanting to complete their packing. Margery was to have a lift to the station in St Austell from Rory, who would be here soon after eight to collect his father.

Nicole was sorry to see them go, especially at this early hour, because the empty day stretched ahead of her in a way she was dreading. Unhappy thoughts were dragging her down as she stripped beds and then made them up again.

All those years ago, Connor had left her of his own volition, and she had thought it was forced on him by her beloved grandparents. She hadn't loved them any the less, but she had believed they were capable of such an unfeeling act. How could she have done that, knowing them as she did? It was an act of betrayal.

Just after eleven-thirty, she locked the front door behind her and walked down to the Post Office. An enquiry for a

B&B had come by the morning post and needed a reply straight away. Her correspondent was very hard of hearing, and so couldn't be dealt with on the phone. She didn't have a computer either.

Nicole avoided glancing at the stone hut across the lane. Time enough to do the cleaning in there later when she checked with Connor that the course next week was still on, in spite of the few bookings.

Daniel's van was parked outside the Post Office. He looked as if he was leaning on it waiting for her, but his surprise to see her was evident.

'You've been saying things about me behind my back,' she accused him.

'I have?'

'To Sophie.'

'What's she been saying now?' His amused expression infuriated her.

'D'you really think I'm unable to cope?'

He straightened. 'Did I say that?'

'Something like it.'

'I merely commented that you looked tired. I'm concerned, that's all, as one friend to another. I think someone's taking you for granted, using you . . .'

A wave of anger that shook her. She swayed a little and caught hold of the car for support.

He opened the passenger door. 'Get in,' he ordered.

His terse tone worked, although she was hardly aware of doing as he said. 'Where are we going? I need to post my letter.'

'It can wait.

'It must catch the post. I can't take her booking for Monday.'

'Why not?

'The stone hut is booked for the next four weeks.'

'What's wrong with the cottage?'

'That too. It's all connected. I can't let the rooms to anyone else. I promised. But no one's coming . . .'

His lips tightened. 'You're not making much sense.'

The next moment, she found herself

pouring it all out: the lack of bookings, her fear that she couldn't make ends meet, that she would have to leave Polvanion.

And leave the stone hut and Connor too, she thought in dismay.

'I'll get rid of him for you.'

She stared at Daniel, appalled.

'He's no good to you, Nicole, no good at all. He treats people with contempt and deserves all he gets. Look at the way he's been treating poor Minna. Mrs Landon discovered that just in time. She was on the point of offering him a building on a long lease, one she owns in the hotel grounds. It's the space he's been looking for to exhibit his work, but he had to go and mess up his chances of getting it. He was livid when he discovered who will have it instead. Now he's spreading ugly rumours.'

'About you?'

'That's the size of it.'

'So you've managed to get round Mrs. Landon instead?'

'She has offered it to me of her own free will, yes.'

She glared at him. 'I don't believe you.'

'You don't have to. I just ask that you keep away from that man. His contract with you isn't worth the paper it's written on.' He looked at her closely. 'If you *have* got a written contract, that is. No? Your expression says it all, Nicole. As I said, I'll get rid of him for you before he does any more harm.'

'That's outrageous. You've no right to say such things. I shall honour my contract with Connor, written or otherwise, and that's all I've got to say. Stay away from me, Daniel. I don't want to see you again.'

She felt for the door handle, and the next moment was out on the road. Daniel was out too, trying to stop her, but she was too quick for him.

He got back in the van and started the engine.

★　★　★

Back indoors, Nicole looked down at the letter in her hand. She had missed the last collection and it wouldn't be on its way until Monday. Well, it couldn't be helped. If the enquirer had any sense, she would get a friend to phone to check. It would be a waste of time to worry about it.

She made a strong coffee and carried it into the front room to drink, sitting on the window seat and looking across the lane to the stone hut. Daniel was way out of order. Annette would say that it was a clever ruse to get hold of the stone hut for himself. Mrs Landon hadn't said anything to her about letting her building to anyone.

Lunchtime came and went. She collected the dry washing from the line in the garden and plugged in the iron.

At last, when she had almost given up hope, there was a knock on the front door. She flew to open it.

'Connor!'

'As large as life. Couldn't get here before. Things to do. Arrangements to make. I need to pick some things up from across the lane.'

In silence, she collected the key from its hook in the kitchen and led the way across to the stone hut. It was dusky in here because of the fading light from the darkening sky outside.

She turned to face him. 'I thought you'd come earlier.'

He wouldn't quite meet her eyes. 'I've been trying to chivvy up more custom. I've been at the gallery in Truro most of the day. The two elderlies have cancelled, and I can't waste myself on one old man, so he's been cancelled too.'

'So my accommodation isn't needed for next week?'

'Or again. The deal's off. I came to tell you and to collect my gear.' He looked round the room. 'I've left it in a bit of a mess.'

And not only the room, she thought.

'It's been good getting to know you again, Nicole; my long-ago — '

'Playmate,' she said, her voice low.

'And that's all I was.'

He laughed. 'You were just seventeen, if I remember. And a charming girl, if I may say so. We had some fun, didn't we?'

'Fun, yes.' Her own laugh had a good attempt at humour in it.

He moved to the window and picked up her precious conch shell. 'My dear love, Christa,' he said.

There was so much longing in his voice that she didn't doubt he spoke the truth; and his words shot through her with painful intensity, because she hadn't known.

She watched silently as he replaced the shell on the windowsill, gathered his belongings and picked up the four paintings. And when he had gone, she saw that he had left the place so empty she felt bereft.

★　★　★

Later, Nicole left the cottage and took the path towards the beach. An early

245

dusk was dimming the outline of the cliffs. She didn't care that the temperature had dropped or that the seagulls had fallen silent. She needed to be out here on her own, drinking in the peace that she hoped would heal her wounded spirits.

On the other side, out of sight from anyone approaching the beach from the lane past the hotel, she found a flat rock to sit on to watch the incoming tide eat up the hard sand in trickles of gentle foam.

Connor had made no promises to her — apart from booking the stone hut and her accommodation for several summer weeks. She had allowed herself to dwell on the past, to attempt to live in a fool's paradise. It was bitter to think of; but if she were honest with herself, it was true. And she had always prided herself on being honest. Annette would vouch for that.

She thought back to her last summer here, and the romantic illusions her seventeen-year-old self had treasured.

And, foolishly, she had allowed herself the same illusions now. She should have known better.

Knowing that Christa had been Connor's true love had no power to hurt her now. Christa had hardly ever spoken of him, so it was likely to have been one-sided. When she had gone to live with her, unhappy because of Connor, Christa had sympathised with her as only she knew how. Her grandparents hadn't betrayed her in the way she had assumed, either.

At last, Nicole stood up, stiff from sitting so long in one position. Rain began to fall, gently at first, and then in a sudden downpour. A flash of lightning lit up the sky. Thunder rumbled. Head down, Nicole ran. She reached the Shack and ran for shelter through the open doorway, and stood gasping for a moment before she saw in another flash of lightning that someone was standing by the bar.

'Minna?'

'The electricity's off. I've been

looking for a torch,' Minna said.

She switched it on, and in its beam Nicole saw the traces of tears on her face.

'Minna, what's wrong?'

'It's definite. We're losing it. Dad had the official letter of notice today.'

'The Shack?'

'Dad's going to retire, he said.'

'But, you?'

'I've loved it here. I wanted it to go on and on, selling our lovely pasties. People come here specially to have them, and . . . ' She took a gasp of air. 'And Connor's leaving. He said . . . But he's gone. I thought . . . ' She was in tears again now, her shoulders shaking.

Nicole put her arm round her, then led her to a stool and perched on another beside her. 'I know, I know.'

'You too?'

'I've been a fool, that's all. I didn't know it until too late.'

*Too late.* The words were like a knell. She had left it too late to value Daniel's friendship in the way he deserved.

248

And now poor Minna was suffering, and she didn't know what to do to help except sit here with her and utter little platitudes. The council wanted to demolish the hut to return the beach to how it had been in the past. But was the past always better than the present? Not for the people who enjoyed the pasties; or for Minna, who liked selling them.

At last Minna's sobs subsided and she raised a tear-stained face. The thunder was fading away too, and there was no longer the rain pounding on the roof.

# 16

Nicole was only vaguely aware of the rumbles of thunder during the night. She had fallen asleep almost immediately after getting into bed. The faint noise in the distance only registered as thunder when a picture of Minna's unhappy face came into her mind. Minna had been upset at Connor's leaving without a word of farewell, but it was the threatened loss of the Shack that was truly devastating for her.

It was said that it wasn't what happened to you in life, but how you coped with it, which strengthened you in ways you never imagined. She hoped that losing the Shack would strengthen Minna; that she could find another venue that would suit her selling of pasties just as well, and would make even more of a success with it.

But . . . wait a minute!

Nicole sat up in bed as an idea shot into her mind. It was too late to offer Daniel the stone hut because he had found somewhere else. But why shouldn't Minna have it? It would do some good for somebody, and that wasn't a bad thing. But would selling pasties there turn out to be illegal too?

She would have to check the position before she made the offer to Minna, and she wanted to do that as soon as possible.

At breakfast time, earlier than usual for a Sunday, Nicole came to a decision. Only yesterday she had told Daniel that she never wanted to see him again. Today she must find him and ask most humbly for his help. If he refused, it would be understandable, and she would have to accept it.

First, though, she went across to the stone hut, carrying the beautiful carving of the seagull on its rock to place on the windowsill as she had promised. It looked well there, side by side with Christa's shell, both items given to her by people she had loved and lost. She looked at them for a long moment and then left.

The morning was calm and peaceful after the storm of yesterday. Across the bay, Chapel Head was misty in the pearly distance, and the sea was like silk.

She walked down to the harbour and saw Daniel's boat attached to the quay. It seemed that he would soon be off in it to discover what the storms had thrown up on beaches along the coast. She wished she was going with him.

And then he came closer, and stopped still in surprise at seeing her.

'I need your help, Daniel,' she said humbly.

She couldn't quite read his expression as she waited for his answer.

'You think I can help you?' he said at last.

'On a legal matter. I want to offer the use of the stone hut to Minna.'

'You do?'

'She needs somewhere else to sell her pasties. I need to know if it would be legal for her to sell them in the stone hut.'

'And you think I'm the right person to ask?'

'I know it.'

'Well, then, yes is my answer. Outside, too, if the weather's kind.'

'You're sure?'

'It was used years ago as a relaxation place for fishermen. I expect you've heard of that?'

She nodded.

'There was a sort of bar there for the selling of food and drink. There would be no change of use now because of that. I'm ninety-nine percent sure, but I'll check with Dad this afternoon.'

'Thank you,' she said.

'Is that all?'

'It's a big *all*, Daniel. I want to help her. I knew you were the person to ask. At first I wanted it as a memorial to my godmother, Christa, who died; she loved the place. Until Connor came, that is, but now he's gone.'

'And left you, just like that?' He eyes

were like gimlets, and she knew her reply was of the utmost importance to him.

'Connor means nothing to me,' she said.

'It's over?'

'It was never on, not really.'

For a moment she was unable to speak because of the tears in her throat. She wanted to tell him how she regretted her hurtful words, but it was impossible. She was afraid to look at him for the contempt she might see in his face, but she owed him an apology at least.

'I'm sorry, Daniel,' she whispered at last. 'I've been a fool.'

'No, Nicole,' he said. 'Never that.' His voice had softened and she dared to look up now.

'And the stone hut still means a lot to you?' he said.

'It always will, because of Christa.'

'And it can be a memorial to her still. Minna will use it during the summer season, but it's still your stone hut; just doing someone else some good in the here and now.'

This was a good thought, and she smiled.

'I'd like to see inside it and offer some suggestions, if I may?

'Of course.'

As they walked up the lane, she was conscious of his nearness in a way she hadn't been before. At the stone hut, she propped the door open and they went inside.

He stood in the centre of the room and looked round. He didn't comment on the mess after the art course. Instead, he drew attention to the good points: the wood-burning stove, plenty of space for a bar and tables as well as a microwave cooker, and somewhere to keep the food warm when the electricity had been laid on.

Then he walked to the window.

'The seagull looks well on the sill,' he said. 'And what's this?' He picked up the conch shell and held it to his ear just as Christa had loved to do.

His face brightened. 'That's wonderful. The magic sound of the sea that puts everything into perspective.'

That was exactly it, Nicole thought, and the reason Christa had liked the shell so much.

'I think I've come to my senses at last,' she said.

Daniel moved closer. 'I came to them the first time I saw you lying on the beach. That's the moment I fell so deeply in love that I knew that life would never be the same for me again.'

'You can't fall in love with someone who's asleep.'

'I did,' Daniel said.

She gazed at him, and sudden joy swept through her. He was looking at her with such love that she knew she wasn't dreaming. This was true, really true. She took the shell from him and held it to her ear. Then she placed it with care on the windowsill next to his seagull, and turned to face him.

For a moment he did nothing. Then she was in his arms.

'I love you, Nicole,' he murmured. 'You believe me?' And he kissed her.

'Always,' she said as she broke away at last. 'I'll always believe in you.'

'Even about setting up business over there in Mrs Landon's precious building, that we both can share?'

'That too. She's a good friend to you.'

'And to you. We'll go from strength to strength. Our children will . . . '

'Surely make their own decisions?'

He laughed. 'Just as we will make our own decision to marry and stay in this place we both love.'

She thought about first hearing of Mrs Landon in Daniel's tiny workroom all those weeks ago. So much had happened since, and now her life was falling into place with a certainty she was not sure she deserved.

They went outside to sit on the bench in the sunshine at the back of the stone hut. With Daniel's arm round her, and with her head on his shoulder, Nicole knew for certain that it was the present that was important. Christa's legacy from the past had been the means of ensuring a happy future.